Insiders

Channing Belle Grove

ISBN: 978-1495947490
ISBN-13: 1495947491

DEDICATION

To Brett, Blair, Sam, Sammy, Jack, Maya and little Peyton Randolph

CONTENTS

ACKNOWLEDGMENTS

Thanks to Melodie, Mary and Margie. You told me what I needed to hear.

1 THE HOMEMAKER

Plain, old fashioned, greed came to Mountain Empire, Virginia before the danger ever did. The first five churches in our county were organized by my seven times great grandfather in 1746. The first official settlement of the city of Mountain Empire was in 1747. You would think after all that time we could have adjusted to a few new people. It wasn't a few though. We had so many new people move here it darn near felt like an invasion. How I wish Washington D.C wasn't such a short drive from this once darling village. Those beltway "incomers" are chiefly to blame for trying to ruin our town like they ruined northern Virginia. It seemed as if the presence of incomers brought us nothing but trouble. They seemed to attract disaster and were frequently part of mayhem and mishap as victims of household accidents. The first one seemed plausible but the second one was suspicious to say the least. After the smoke cleared my radar was tuned. Maybe the myriad of their injuries really were a fluke- - as they appeared to be.

But, in my opinion……. did they ever happen to some deserving people. Someone could have been killed in all of the situations. One of the folks is still not out of the woods yet. Suffice it to say, no one leaves their doors unlocked like we used to. You won't find a key in any of the obvious places either. Before the incomers arrived, we had the kind of community where you could call on a neighbor at the drop of a hat. It didn't matter if you needed a shoulder to cry on or someone to let the cat out in a pinch. There wasn't a soul here that wouldn't wave in passing. Our former ways worked best for everyone. Now, I am a young seventy but still of that generation who wears white only after Easter and never after Labor Day. I'm going to stick with my tried and true bob and only a touch of makeup too. There is no reason to change what works is what I say. That philosophy is what motivates me to insist on keeping my hometown like it was. You could go as far as to say I am determined by all definition to get my town back to some semblance of what we used to call normal.

One of my longtime Mountain Empire friends remarked to me one day,

"Tiggy, we have become a refugee center for folks from New York, New Jersey, Washington, D.C., Pennsylvania, and all over God's half acre."

I must take that a step further. More than a few of the incomers may even be here as part of the Witness Protection Plan. After all, we are only a few hours from the nation's capital where those kinds of arrangements are made. We at the Hill and Dale Bridge Club believe they have all done something illegal before moving here. It doesn't seem plausible this many seemingly affluent people, with no real job are really upstanding citizens. I don't buy their pretentious lifestyles are supported by working from home on a silly computer. I may be "old school", but it still takes honest work to make an honest dollar.

Incomers claim it was the small town atmosphere and lack of traffic jams which attracted them. But I know part of the reason Mountain Empire was selected is really the fact houses were so much cheaper here. I don't buy it was the Blue Ridge Mountains and the scenery attracting them. No, it was the way their "greenery" stretched farther here after selling their generic homes up north. One former New York Times reporter had just settled in when her neighbor casually asked her if she had found a church to attend. She is one of those women who looks all one shade of gray, with a sock puppet mouth when she talks. The lady was insulted to the nth degree and practically growled at our poor citizen. An honest attempt at helping the new woman meet people was considered a hostile act.

"That would never happen in New York because half the town is Jewish."

To which our fair citizen replied, "My dear, I am not a member of the WE'RE THE ONLY ONES GOING TO HEAVEN CHURCH. In fact I consider myself a member of the NO ONE GOES TO HELL UNLESS THEY WANT TO church. Besides, I was only trying to be friendly!"

The lady was stuck in that New York state of mind (suspicious of everything). She had no idea in small town Virginia- all Synagogues, tent meetings or reciting the

Apostle's Creed, fall into the category of *church*. For goodness sakes, we even have one of those churches here now where they pray "to whom it may concern." It's still church, though, and that's the point.

Before the incomers moved in, house prices and rentals in this town were affordable to anyone. Nobody went hungry, with jobs available at the state mental hospital, the school for the deaf and blind, Mountain Laurel College, Stuart Hall for girls, two military schools, and lots of farms in the county. The huge old Victorian homes in town used to be recycled to the children and grandchildren of the original owners. But that was before the centuries old Mental Hospital closed, the military academies folded and the hospital moved out to the county. As much as it costs to heat an old house it's no wonder none of the original families wanted to live in one. We were all ripe for plucking after that.

Right in the wake of that, the highway exit was completed out by our old state road. Then an All Mart opened up at the highway exit and the businesses uptown barely held on by the hair of their chinny chin chin.

In February of 1988, the old guard in the oldest houses on the main streets died out in record numbers. One by one the "painted ladies" as we used to call them, sat empty, overgrown and abandoned. You let a wisteria vine go more than three years and it will take over the whole house. The established gardens of the older homes around me were becoming a monument to neglect. The wonderful old hedges, azaleas and hydrangeas were once a source of pride to the whole town. Gospel Hill and Sherwood Ave, where I lived included close to six square blocks of serene order. Before the incomers, Sherwood Ave was where everyone came for Halloween. Christmas time, our light displays were the tour of choice on Christmas Eve. Local parents brought their children every year like clockwork. Santa Claus secretly put many a bike together while children all freshly bathed and pajama-ed were driven through the Gospel Hill area on Christmas Eve.

By 1992, our long time mayor soon announced his upcoming retirement. Next thing I knew, the city council passed resolutions condemning four of the biggest and grandest "ladies" in my neck of the woods. Shelby Ann Wytheville was the first realtor to get the bright idea of running ads in the large northern cities showcasing those homes for sale. Her grandmother told me it was just a trial balloon to see what kind of response she would get. Apparently, one Sunday's run in the classifieds of the New York Times and Washington Post got one hundred and twenty four responses. All the homes were advertised way above what she planned to offer the owners. That was Shelby Ann though, sharp as a tack. She was a hundred and seven pounds of red hair, big blue eyes and fearless as a grizzly bear. Her very own grandmamma once described Shelby Ann as a Mack truck disguised like a Volkswagen. That could explain why she never married.

Several of us in the Hill and Dale were guffawing privately over anybody thinking those houses deemed unsafe by the city would ever sell. As my friend and fellow member, Estelle Gwaltney put it,

"If the termites ever unclasp hands, you know those old places left empty on West Beverley would probably fall to the ground."

Let me hasten to add that I am a Beverley descendant. My Beverley ancestor married a Randolph, which is the family of Thomas Jefferson's mother. So, of course I care about the town looking as well as possible. I just didn't want unsavory people taking over. I wouldn't exactly describe the incomers as carpetbaggers, more like "rug traders". I guess we in the Hill and Dale were oblivious to just how desperate people were in the large northern cities to own a home and a piece of land. Before telling anybody how many had responded to her ads, dear Shelby Ann quickly offered the descendants on the deeds of four Victorians slated for demolition, forty thousand dollars apiece. Even Shelby's grandmother was in the dark about the potential buyers she had waiting in the wings. No doubt each and every one of the descendants figured the repairs and heating costs would have put a child through the University of Virginia in style. They sold to Shelby quietly and gratefully. What a con job she did on them.

I often think back on the irony of what folks in town first thought about the sale of those pretty, old home places. People kept saying how lucky it was that Shelby Ann could buy them up and stop the wrecking ball. That was the consensus at a meeting of the Hill and Dale garden club too. Someone asked me at that meeting, "Tiggy, isn't it mahvelous?" All I could think was what realtor does anything out of the goodness of their heart? Our meeting was at Lib Wytheville's, Shelby Ann's grandmother. I decided to keep my doubts between me and the lamp post. I tossed my long bob back and batted my baby blues like nobody's business. But I darn near locked my jaw with secret fury.

Within weeks of Shelby Ann's first home selling for sixty two thousand, Miss Shelby hired a couple of former tobacco pickers to give her three other "vintage" properties a lick and a promise at staging them to sell. All she had them do was slap a coat of paint on the front and put a few air fresheners out. Then the "Homemaker" (that's what her signs said) placed more ads in the Washington Post, New York Times and Philadelphia Enquirer. I found out later the ads simply said, Authentic Eastlake Victorian, on quarter of an acre with original charm, offered from one hundred twenty five thousand dollars. That translates into: not a darn thing had been done to them in years. In all my born days, we in Mountain Empire have never been hoity toity enough to call a Gingerbread house an Authentic Eastlake. How put on!

Pretentious or not, once again Shelby had an unbelievable response. Shelby's broker, Martha Lofton, bragged about it in line at the grocery store. Dear Martha was never one of my favorite people and I felt like that from pure instinct. She would go to funerals and hand out her business card. I'd bet money she attended the services just to ask the grieving widow or widower to call her if they decided to sell their houses. If I give her the benefit of the doubt, it would be because real estate in this town was not a money making project for the longest time. Martha didn't work to sell anything. Once the owner dropped the price at her panicked urging, the house sold. I know of no one who felt they ever got service after the sale from her.

I remember the marquis in front of First Presbyterian that Wednesday read: Blessed are the meek, for they shall inherit the earth. Little did we know, it was yuppies with cash and the "Homemaker" who would be getting so much of ours. As for me, I just hoped we wouldn't start getting over run and overpriced for our own good. Little did I know that would be the least of our worries once those incomers began moving in.

After dear Shelby's ads ran it wasn't long before we all encountered cars from New York, New Jersey and Washington, D.C. The passengers were ones that didn't wave back. Lib Wytheville complained about this to Shelby in front of Estelle Gwaltney. Estelle called me the day Lib was snubbed.

"Tiggy, I Suwannee, Lib waved to some folks from New Jersey and they looked at her like she was from a different planet!" Foot traffic uptown was starting to pick up at the same time. At least the so and so's parked their fancy cars and made time to shop and eat uptown.

The Lick Skillet café and the old Johnson Hotel were the only places to eat downtown. A few years earlier, our longtime mayor made sure fast food places were relegated to the highway exit by the All Mart. That was when we all had enough fight left in us to deal with lawyers so slick they were greasy. The old hotel was built in 1854, it was called the Johnson after Andrew Johnson. I'm pretty sure the last time it was remodeled was after World War II. It was the green stamp pictures added in 1964 to the rooms and the formal dining area that I could have done without.

Soon, the second home sale went through for a hundred twenty five thousand dollars. It was as if incomers were willing to pay any asking price, never checking to see what the property was assessed at. Then again, an honest realtor should have done that for them. Everyone at church was buzzing at the amazing price the second home had sold for. Reverend Steven's wife remarked to some ladies after services soon after.

"Shelby Ann says these incomers want old homes. She calls it historic property."

I had to say my piece. "This uptown is mostly historic property if you consider the newest homes were built during the Great Depression. All of our property taxes could go up if those prices continue." Mrs. Reverend Steven's gave me a look as if I had threatened to out Santa Claus.

The marquis in front of the church that week was from second Corinthians, chapter five. I was on my way uptown but I slowed down long enough to read it without having to park. "Now we know that if the earthly tent we live in is destroyed, we have a building from God, an eternal house in heaven, not built by human hands." Just as I finished reading it, a car came up behind me and honked. It was one of those huge SUV's with a Washington, D.C. tag. I wished just that once I had put a bumper sticker on my car. As a rule, I avoid things like that. But if I'd had one that day, it would have read: Tourist Season is open and I'm loaded for bear. I would put a picture of a woman on the sticker, blowing on the barrel of a fancy pistol.

The first family to move into my neighborhood bought the old Varney place. Every time I walked my little dog past their house, there was a different truck parked there. I saw vans with a plumber's logo, or some kind of repair service in front, on the lawn and in the back. It looked for all the world to see, they were living in one room of the house for the longest time. My handy man Woody, had sons who did electric work and carpentry, they were jack of all trades. Woody came to hang one of those sensor lights at my garage door. As usual, I found something else for him to fix. While repairing the sliding channel on the kitchen door, he told me all about the people in the old Varney home.

"Woody, I guess your boys are making a pretty penny right about now."

"Yes Ma'am, the people what bought the Varney place are having it rewired, replumbed, refinishing the floors and that ain't all."

A few days after he told me that, I had a hamburger for lunch at the Lick Skillet cafe. Hazel, the owner of the café, served it with a side of fries and fresh information. She leaned over and said in a whisper tone, "Whada-ya reckon those folks have already spent on the old Varney place?"

"I'm sure I don't know, but for darn sure more than it's worth."

"More than a hundred thousand- -and they say they're adding central air next."

"Hazel, why in the world wouldn't they replace the roof first, it must be old as Methuselah."

"Oh I spose that'll be next. Vicky, that's Mrs. Snickelfritz, told me they are going to put a new metal roof on to make it period. And that is gonna cost close to forty thousand! They talk a lot about period this and period that."

"Well, metal roofs sound good when it rains but they are expensive nowadays, *period*! How ostentatious can you get! Nobody, and I mean nobody with any semblance of breeding talks about how much money they've spent on their house. Not even close friends should do that."

She laughed.

"Tiggy, I would rather have a shingle roof myself cause it's so much cheaper."

"Well Hazel you sound like you kinda know these, whosamajigs, mmmmm...... could you say their last name again?"

"It's Snickelfritz, and yeah, I've gotten to know them a little Tiggy. They haven't had a kitchen to speak of since they moved in. They warm a seat here three meals a day a lot of times."

"Nobody else has yet to hear a peep out of them. Maybe I'll stop by with a welcome dinner tomorrow."

"Tiggy, that'd be real nice. I'm sure they'll appreciate it."

The next day, I went to the super All Mart out by the highway. I bought the ingredients for a sheet cake, a whole fryer and some puny looking green beans. I got busy cookin' and made enough extra to freeze. You never know when you might be called on to take food in this town. I tried several times to call the Snickelfritzes but got nothing but an answering machine. What the heck I thought, they'll appreciate a home cooked dinner. I decided to drop in before supper time and present my offering of welcome. Just as daylight started to wane, I was walking up the familiar slate path to the Varney place. It seemed the yard was last on their list, but it was early fall. Til all the leaves are down it's a waste of time to rake anyway. For a moment, I was a child, trick or treating at the Varneys. It was years ago and yet it was yesterday all at the same time. Old Mrs. Varney lost her husband in 1932 and her boys had to work for the WPA to support the family. Work Projects Administration was responsible for building the walls and camp grounds on the Blue Ridge Parkway. I could see Mrs. Varney clear as day with her Marcel waved hair. Her hair was streaked with grey and silver, looking as plaid as her skirt. She wore a grey cardigan and sturdy shoes until the first of April.

I reached the porch with my heirloom tray full of aluminum foil wrapped food. I looked around, still amazed at the big columns and the air of gentility the porch reflected. I knocked on the door, assuming the door bell was still broken. Then I noticed a New York Times still in its wrapper by the door. Mr. Snickelfritz came to the door, "Hullo." He said as he reached for the paper.

"Hey there, I'm your neighbor catty corner behind you." I could tell he wasn't sure what I meant.

"Well, you look like your arms are full, I'm Bert Snickelfritz."

His voice was loud and his body looked like he'd been cut off at the knees. He couldn't have been any taller than me and I'm not quite five foot two. He spoke so loudly, I wondered if maybe he might be hard of hearing or thought I was. As he opened the door for me, the wife appeared from the back hall with a friendly but curious look.

"How do y'all do, I'm your neighbor and thought y'all could do with some home cookin."

"You didn't have to do that" she said in a friendly voice. I took her for genuine and asked where she would like me to put the tray. It was getting heavy.

"Ohhhh, I'm sorry. Bert, take the tray from the nice lady." She said it in a chastising tone. You'd of thought she was auditioning for teacher's pet.

"Of course, what was I thinking!"

I knew right then and there these folks were out of their element. They were awkwardly social, almost robotic as they tried to make a good impression. I took in the surroundings as discreetly as possible. They must have spent a fortune on antiques. I have never had to buy any of my antiques. The Snickelfritzes had staged the interior with the theme of "Early Country Store". I've no doubt the expression on my face looked like someone had thrown a bucket of ice water at me.

Vicky Snickelfritz said proudly, "As you can see we have made a lot of changes."

"You certainly have."

Let me tell you the lady of the house wasn't exaggerating. Gone was the eclectic mix of furnishings handed down and family portraits back several generations. In its place were reproduction metal posters of baking flour and table syrup. The only prop missing from the country store theme was a working cash register.

"Would you like to see the renovations we have made so far?" I graciously offered, "If it's not any trouble."

Bert and Vicky took me through the entire house, both competing with each other as they pointed out the works in progress. I could see each room was decorated with what I call a "country cute" theme. Vicky Snickelfritz described it as "primitive".

The only way I can convey the overall look would be; Pig in a Poke and distressed at best. Each bathroom had been enlarged and redone in what can only be termed; Victorian factory direct. "Claw foot tubs must be all the rage." I left out the fact I had never seen a claw foot tub with stainless steel claws. I casually asked the couple if they planned to work in the area. Mr. Snickelfritz said, "I'll be managing a franchise business my father bought. The new Ye Olde Pickle Barrel restaurant, out by the highway exit."

"Oh, how nice for you. Did you bring this furniture with you from New York?"

Vicky piped up, "We got most of it at estate auctions." Sometimes people who haven't made their own living tend to have little imagination. Then again, the restaurant franchise he owned looked very much like their home. You know the kind, they are at every major highway exit from New Jersey to Florida. Usually they are named things like, Mama's All You Can Eat or

Country Cupboard. On the entry wall were black and white photos of pioneer looking people.

"Is that some of your family?"

"No, those are just some portraits we bought at an antique store."

Imagine my shock at the sight of instant ancestors! No amount of money in this world can buy someone else's heritage, but I let that presumption go without a word from me. No sir-ree, decent people know blood will always tell. The family tree bought at retail, certainly gave new meaning to the phrase: identity theft.

Then the husband put his two cents in.

"This is the color we are going to paint the house."

He spoke briskly, hardly letting you hear a vowel. I certainly hoped he didn't have the audacity to make fun of my southern accent. He talked like he had a fire to go to. Bert Snickelfritz was beaming from ear to ear as he held the paint swatches in his hand like a straight flush.

Vicky piped in as she pointed to the paint swatches, "The color is called Heather on the Gray, an authentic Victorian color."

That spoke volumes to me. These people sporting a last name with too many consonants for a name tag at church, obviously thought they were going to be lords of the manor as soon as the paint dried. All that crossed my mind was, Victorian color aside, they were going to paint this beautiful old home- Easter Egg purple. I couldn't help wondering if they even observed the holiday. I certainly wasn't going to invite them to my church and get a reaction like that New York woman.

I must say the Snickelfritzes were friendly enough.

"Well, y'all have certainly been busy. I hope I haven't kept you."

Bert and Vicky walked me out peppering questions about who I would suggest for this or that home repair. I feigned ignorance and left with a smile and good wishes. I was not about to give away my longstanding helpers. I walked home thinking I would need to put the heat on soon. It was getting nippy. I called my handyman Carter Crawford as soon as I got home. I wanted to make sure I was on his list for getting my furnace serviced.

"I'll get to you sometime tomorrow between sun up and dark thirty." Typical of Carter not to commit to a time. I told him the back door would be open in case I wasn't there. At that time, there was no need to lock up during the day.

"Yesum, thank you."

The house across from me sold right before Christmas that year. It had been the home of a longstanding friend of mine. A couple from Florida bought it, but I never did get the name of the town. Come to think of it, when I asked they answered with a question about Mountain Empire. Thinking back, I was off my game to have let that go. I only went over to introduce myself and offer any help I could. They had no children and I would guess they were in their early forties. After I introduced myself, he told me he was terrible with names.

"Let's just keep it simple, I'm John and this is Joanna." Joanna was friendly enough to ask me for any good recipes I had. I promised to give her my turkey in a sack recipe. I later heard from Estelle, who heard it from Lib, that he had inherited money. Estelle said they bought the house through the local probate judge with cash. My friend who previously owned it had died childless. There was something familiar about the new owners, but I couldn't put my finger on it.

I was at Bridge Club when the subject came up about these people having that much cash.

Lilly Wiley asked, "Tiggy, have you met your new neighbors?" "I introduced myself day before yesterday." Estelle Gwaltney asked what their names were.

"All I know is John and Joanna. He's teaching at Stuart Hall and she teaches at the Deaf and Blind School. They have no children and they told me they want to keep the house as close to the same as possible."

"Law!", rang out from all around me.

Lilly said, "You mean they're not gonna rip out walls, take down all the curtains and paint the inside with toilet brushes and feather dusters?"

We all laughed at that. So far, every incomer was taking all the charm out of the homes. In its place, were what they called period this and Zen that. Every jack leg painter in the county was claiming the ability to paint "faux" finishes. It was a hoot to listen to incomers in the hardware store asking where the "Jewel" tone paint colors were. You can call a shade a jewel tone, but it's still a primary color to me. Lilly then held her bridge hand close, "Pass."

"I'm going to take supper over like I did for the people that bought the old Varney Place."

Everyone remarked without looking up.

"That's nice."

I couldn't help wondering how it would be to have John and Joanna in Mattie Fisher's home. She was also a former member of the Hill and Dale. Mattie died of a stroke the previous year at the age of seventy-two. Her late ex-husband was on the deed but the house was paid for long before he left her. Mattie was given the option to split the profits after its sale or have life estate at her divorce from John. She couldn't afford to move and didn't want to anyway. After she died, her late ex-husband's half of the sale went to his son I suppose. Mattie was only a year older than me and had enjoyed poor health. I was careful not to ask her how she felt unless I had the time and the constitution to listen. Her mainstay of life was getting attention with health problems from her church and circle of friends and neighbors. She had more imaginary aches and pains then the Pope has Catholics. It was never anything an X-ray or blood test could find.

Her husband ran off with her first cousin, named Halcey Ann. Halcey Ann came from Tampa, Florida to visit Mattie every Christmas if she was between husbands. Mattie's husband John was Halcey Ann's fourth and final husband. John and Halcey Ann had one son and no other children. When the son was nine, John and Halcey Ann were killed in a bizarre car accident in Tampa. The accident was caused when someone moved a big bulldozer from the side of the road to a blind spot in the middle of the road. Halcey Ann and John were the only ones in the car. The son went to live with Halcey Ann's parents after the tragedy. I assumed the boy had a good life, since his grandfather was a Methodist minister. Mattie provided no other information about him after that. I know Mattie would love to have had children but she never remarried. She had a long time love affair with her medical encyclopedia after John Fisher left her. If she had ever gotten on the internet to research all her imagined symptoms she would have felt even sicker.

I had no more gotten in the door from bridge club that afternoon when Lilly Wiley called me.

"You are not going to believe what I heard!" she gasped through the phone.

"Ye Gods and little catfishes; Lilly; just tell me nobody has died!"

"Oh no, nothing like that." It's just that Shelby Ann has sold the other two houses of hers. One sold for a hundred and fifty thousand and the other for two hundred fifty thousand!"

"You can't be serious, those houses are barely on a half-acre!" I caught my breath. "Lilly, what is happening to this town?"

"I tell you what Tiggy, the first person that offers me anywhere near that, I'm moving to an apartment over by the post office."

"And Lilly, just what do you think your two Best in Show Corgis will do for a yard?"

"Oh Tiggy, you're right. After Walter died, I don't know what I would have done if it hadn't been for my babies. Tiggy, you know Jenny and Beaucoup have won in their category for twelve straight years."

Oh dear Lord in Heaven, I thought. Here we go again. Those dogs didn't know they were dogs. Everybody knew not to enter that house of hers wearing stockings- -or short pants. I dearly loved my little dog Pookie, but I wasn't willing to haul her around to every podunk town for dog shows like Lilly did with her two Corgis. "Lilly, are you forgetting I'm the one who saves you the write up every time?" She laughed.

"You have always let me have my little claim to fame." "Lilly, are you sure Shelby Ann really sold that property for those outrageous prices?"

"Oh it's the gospel truth, I got it from Lib herself." Lib lived a block down from me. I suwannee, she trimmed her boxwoods with fingernail scissors before dawn every day in the summer. They have stayed the same manicured and elegant entrance to her house for forty years.

"Lib says Shelby Ann is the top selling realtor in the county."

I smiled through my teeth. "She's a real go getter."

"What do realtors make off sales like that?"

"She has to share some part of it with her broker, Lilly. Martha Lofton probably gets a hefty percentage of everything."

"I know Lib is proud don't you Tiggy?"

"Yes Lilly. I guess we'll be seeing those HomeMaker signs everywhere soon."

"Well, it couldn't happen to a nicer girl from a nicer family."

With great restraint I said, "Oh absolutely Lil." Then we said our goodbyes and hung up.

Right there, with only The Almighty in ear shot, I lost my cool, "Home Maker my foot, that girl is gonna drive up taxes out the wazoo! Doesn't she care we are trying to live off pensions and Social Security? Home Wrecker is more like it!"

Then it dawned on me, the old Chapman place and the Elwood Stevens the III house were both within spitting distance of Lib Wytheville. I smiled at the thought of two more families from God only knows what background, living that close to Miss First Families of Augusta County. Dear Shelby would get a good dose of what for if Lib didn't like her new neighbors. So far, these incomers were so new rich acting, they stuck out like a fly in a bowl of buttermilk.

The next Sunday, I was setting up the coffee pot at First Presbyterian when Lib Wytheville stopped for a cup.

"How do you like your new neighbors Lib?"

She got a slightly strained look on her face as she tried to smile. "Why fine, but they are a little different."

"Oh, in what way?" Of course I was thinking to myself, different bad I'll just bet. Then Lib caught my attention.

"Well, one of them at least speaks English. They are from New York. All they talked about was Manhattan this and Manhattan that."

"Well what's their name?"

"It's spelled Puckett, but the wife corrected me and pronounced it "Pookay"."

"Ha! You can call a person "pookay" but they're still a Puckett." Lib giggled for a moment.

"Tiggy they bragged about selling their Brownstone for over a million dollars, can you believe that?"

"Oh sure, people up there pay monthly fees for a parking spot that equals our social security check." I'll tell you one thing Lib, if they think you can make a living down here like in New York, they've got a rude awakening coming."

"Well Tiggy, according to Mr. "Pookay", they are retiring here to live off investments from the sale of the Brownstone. That is, after they fix the house up."

"Good Lord, what else needs to be done, other than a little paint and hedge trimming?"

"Tiggy, I can just tell, these people have money for the first time in their life and they are gonna wear it like a badge. By the way, they have a son almost through school, so I offered to make some introductions for him. He seemed like a nice boy. He is the wife's child not the husband's."

"Oh, well that was nice of you Lib."

"That's all I know for now."

"That sounds alright Lib, what did you mean by them being different?"

Lib looked at me and leaned in as if she were giving away state secrets. "It's the other family in the Elwood Stevens house that are more than a little different."

"How so?"

"My dear, they claim to be from D.C. but they are certainly not from there originally. Their last name looks like something off of the DMV eye chart. Take my word for it, they have close relatives overseas, if you get my drift. They speak very broken English. I have counted more people in that house than you can shake a stick at Tiggy. I spoke to the husband as he was talking to Woody Jr. on the side of the house. (Woody Lamb Jr. had a small construction business.) Mr. Whatchamacallit, told me his family includes a wife, four kids, his mother, his uncle and aunt and maybe a nephew will join them."

"What pray tell is their name Lib?"

"I tell you Tiggy, I couldn't begin to repeat it the way they say it. I asked the husband to spell it and what a mouthfull. It's spelled Pahnisahndra and sounds like "Pawnysandara". The women of the family smile but have yet to speak. The oddest thing too, is all the women of the family have the same birthmark. Poor things, it's a mole right between their eyes! They all wear these long, wrap around dresses. They are made out of the most colorful material! They have long black hair which is kept under a scarf thingy attached to their dresses."

"What!, I exclaimed as politely and discreetly as possible. "Lib, are they from, …are they A-rabs?"

"Lord only knows Tiggy, but Shelby Ann keeps telling me they are real nice."

"Well Lib, let's just hope they don't speak in the unknown tongue and eat our cats and dogs!"

Within two months, Shelby Ann's aunt decided to sell her stunning old four square. It was built in 1910 and had pretty details on the outside. It was only three bedrooms but it was in good condition. It sold before anyone knew it was on the market for a hundred and eighty five thousand. The house was diagonally two houses across from me. Thankfully the new owners were supposed to be from Kentucky. At least they would speak our language. The couple's name was Hugh and Betty McMinn. He was going to be the new librarian at Mountain Laurel College and Betty was going to work as a secretary. They had a grown daughter that lived in Richmond. Lib found out something a little peculiar about them from Shelby Ann. It was strange enough for her to call me the minute she knew.

"Shelby said the husband had a sweat shirt on when he signed the contract in her office that had Tampa Bay Buccaneers on it. When Shelby asked them if they had ever lived in Tampa the man turned red as a beet. Then, Tiggy, he nudged his wife under the table, not realizing Shelby had that big mirrored wall behind them. Then he said "Oh,…. uh…, I think my wife bought this at a yard sale." Shelby said the man acted like he might be hiding something."

I was distracted for a minute thinking how Shelby Ann probably enjoyed looking at herself in the mirrored wall when she's not busy. I caught myself before I mused out loud.

"Lib, who gives a rat's behind what team he supports?"

"I know Tiggy, but that's not my point. Why would someone get upset and turn red when asked if he ever lived in Tampa? Why would he nudge his wife like he wanted her to back up his story about getting that shirt from a silly yard sale?"

So, I joked back, "Maybe they are from the witness protection plan!"

Lib pressed on with worry in her voice, "Tiggy, don't you think the way he reacted was odd?"

2 HISTORICAL HYSTERIA

After that odd behavior of Hugh McMinn's at the closing of his and Betty's house, Betty got a job as the secretary at Lofton Realty. It seemed the ink had barely dried on their house contract with Shelby Ann. Shelby made a pretty penny on that sale so, no surprise she made a job for Betty. A few months later, Betty got her real estate license and became a realtor for Martha Lofton Realty. This put her in direct competition with Shelby. Next, she got the listing for several farms which sold to developers from Charlottesville. She claimed to be sympathetic to the farmers since she was from Kentucky. We townsfolk began referring to the impending cluster developments as "Marlboro Country Estates" just to irritate the politically correct incomers. Between the price land and homes in town sold for, by the end of 1990, the whole town and surrounding country side was fruit basket turnover. For the first time in fifty years, I could go to the grocery store without running into a soul I knew from longstanding. I felt like a stranger in a town my family had settled before the Revolutionary War. It was unsettling to say the least.

The Panisahndrahs next to Lib Wytheville were not the only people to move here from other countries either. Mr. Krishna something or other, bought the only gas station uptown. It was the only station in town that wasn't entirely self-serve. I just wished he had bought the one out by the highway. What would my late husband have thought about a gas station attendant wearing a blue dish towel around his head? Gopal Panisahndrah took over the restaurant at the old Johnson Hotel. Let me tell you, the entire family worked that restaurant as if their life depended on it. What with a chain restaurant like Ye Olde Pickle Barrel and more coming, The Johnson no longer had a monopoly.

Gopal's mother usually acted as hostess for him. She wore her uniform of the day, which I would classify as a colorful, hippie nightgown. Who knows, maybe where they came from it would be considered a dress fit for a beauty pageant! I guess that's why there's chocolate and vanilla. People have a right to follow their culture, I just preferred they follow it where they came from. Our Confederate History Guild met at the Johnson for lunch the second Tuesday of every month. We couldn't help but admire how hard working *Gopal* and *et al* were. "Mama Sr." Panisahndrah was extremely proud of how she redecorated the ante bellum era restaurant. My secret name for her style of furniture and art was "Mamasutra Kama Sutra". They did treat Lib like a queen whenever she came in and that was very nice.

The wallpaper Mama Sr. Panisahndrah picked was red and white, similar to a toile. Except the figures in the pattern were Greek looking women depicted pouring water on each other while a bunch of togo wearing men looked on. It was like the ancient Greek equivalent of a wet T-shirt contest! The darkened areas on the front of the water toting women left a lot to be desired in a family restaurant. No one but me seemed to notice though. The new furniture they put in the lobby of the old Johnson was reminiscent of the Madam's quarters in Gone With The Wind. gilded and ornate, with red velvet cushions and drapes. It probably came from some place called Discount French Provincial. Fake red rose bouquets were on the entry table. The roses were complete with drops of glue on them to mimic water droplets. The fake roses were at every table with a plastic table cloth no less. It just took my breath away.

The most outlandish display of false elitism from the incomers was their forming the Historical Review Committee. Hugh McMinn was instrumental in organizing the Historical Review Committee (HRC) as it was to become known as. He got a petition signed by every incomer and naive citizen he could to start the committee. He explained what he was forming was similar to an HOA but without a monthly or yearly fee. He organized the incomers to attend town council meetings in order to learn rules required by city ordinances. How Hugh picked up on all the nuances of getting his committee recognized as a legitimate civic organization would have to be admired. That is how the Historical Review Committee slipped by us. Woody Lamb, jack of all trades and master of none, happened to be on the city council when the votes were cast. The council voted overwhelmingly to allow members of the Historical Review Committee to have initial say on building permits in my neighborhood and proposed several other streets to eventually come under its control. Since Woody and his sons had a home repair business, he was all for the HRC.

I have to say, those of us born and raised here were asleep at the wheel to allow a home owners association of that type. Most of us living off retirement incomes soon had a tiger by the tail (figuratively) termed architectural covenants. It didn't dawn on any of us that had owned property for years, the Historical Review Committee could tell *us* what color to paint or what fence was architecturally accurate. None of the citizens were consulted a single iota on the Historical Review Committee's over reaching guidelines. Only incomers were in on those. The paper never made it clear the committee was anything but a group of volunteers who would suggest guidelines for home improvement and upkeep. These incomers were so impressed with themselves they lost sight of the fact they were about to turn Mountain Empire into what they had fled from: high taxes, high priced real estate and devalued community relations.

Martha Lofton, Shelby Ann Wytheville and Betty McMinn were the least of our worries for realtors. Realtors moved here from D.C., Massachusetts, and local rats came up out of the sewer too. The majority of the female realtors that were incomers looked like the wrath of God. They dressed in a style somewhere between flower child and missionary. They mistook the natural look for one I would call weather beaten. I say, if your beauty isn't a work of nature, than make it a work of art.

Every time I picked up the morning paper, I noticed another internet course offering real estate training. Two national real estate companies opened in Mountain Empire with offices downtown and out by the All Mart. They all sang praises that the HRC, (Historic Review Committee) could tell us what we could and could not do with our property. I began making a mental note of who was all for the HRC. I couldn't help thinking of my favorite classic: <u>A Tale Of Two Cities</u>. The most interesting character to me was Madame de Farge. She knitted all day and included the family crest of every evil member of the French aristocracy in her pattern. When it came time to chop off the heads of those who mistreated commoners, it was her knitting that identified the names of the guilty. It's not in me to chop anybody's head off, but there were a few individuals on the Historical "correctness" Committee I would have liked to put in traction.

The way one of our local country boys acted when he went from Bobby Tatum to Tatum Home Improvements was anything but an improvement for Estelle Gwaltney's son- -and I'll get to that. That Bobby Tatum was weird and arrogant at the same time. First of all, the man was from a family known for trashy behavior. There wasn't a one of them that had ever amounted to a hill of beans.

It's safe to say they were known for having the morals of an alley cat. The incomer's all came here with hefty profits from selling overpriced property in the big cities. They didn't quibble over what any local yokel like Bobby charged. Bobby Tatum took advantage of them right and left, and that is a fact.

Carter Crawford, my plumber, had bought up several dumps over the years and rented them out cheaply to needy families under something called Section 8. Even he started selling off any house of his that was remotely "historic". A realtor from a place near Boston bought one of his big old places and turned it into four apartments. Each one rented for a monthly fee more than my social security check. Bobby Tatum was a drinkin buddy of Carter's and they fed each other leads on repair business. Incomers and handy men began taking the Historical Review Committee and themselves way yonder too seriously.

Estelle Gwaltney's son Pete had married a lovely girl he met at Mountain Laurel College. She was from a fine family near Memphis and fit right in from the moment we first met her. Pete didn't make the money she was used to but they did make two beautiful children. Estelle decided to cash in a bond and give Pete and Darla a new kitchen for their tenth anniversary. Bobby Tatum was hired to do the job and he sure did a number on Pete and Darla.

He brought his humongous black dog everywhere he had a job. That monster rode everywhere with him in the back of his truck. One day it chased my neighbor and her little Maltese within an inch of their lives. Bobby refused to do the decent thing and keep it on a leash. If you ask me, he needed to be on a leash himself. Bobby fixed more than Pete and Darla's kitchen. He left his wife shortly after he began "fixing" Darla and Pete's kitchen. However, not before he was seen out with Darla. Then he began attending church with her. I for one tried not to sit close to them on Sunday, just in case lightening decided to strike.

Estelle was absolutely done in when Pete and Darla separated over Mr. Handy man. Pete and Darla divorced by the following spring of 1995. Bobby divorced his wife about the same time. That Easter, our Hill and Dale garden party was held at Estelle's. Pete and Darla's children helped their grandmother serve punch at the fete. I asked the granddaughter how she was doing, trying to make polite conversation. The poor child looked like she had lost her best friend. "Fine," she said and then looked down at her shoes. It would have been awkward to engage her beyond that.

Bobby had lived in a rented shack near the railroad depot before moving into Darla and Pete's old house. He moved in shortly before the party at Estelle's. The house was on the block over from me but it was catty corner behind me. Pete moved into an apartment close to his old house. Next thing I knew, Darla and Bobby were married. I thought it was a bad sign for Darla to have her new husband move in with her. She was doing all the conceding of territory and even let him put his name in the phone book in place of hers. Bobby did nothing but crowd the neighborhood with all of his construction supplies and fishing canoes. The garbage truck had to maneuver around all his stuff each week. He had two of the most beat up trucks for hauling you ever saw. He bought a new car for his personal use and parked in the one car garage where Darla used to park. She now had to park on the street. In the shared alley behind our respective streets, he stacked ladders and buckets, everything but the kitchen sink. The neighbors on either side were not happy about turning our alley into a storage facility and boat dock. One of the neighbors wrote a letter to the editor of the paper complaining about construction equipment hampering our ingress and egress through the city alley. Of course he was too polite to name names as to who was responsible for the inconvenience. Bobby was too selfish to do anything about it even though he knew about the letter in the paper. It was well known around town, Bobby was doing little odd jobs for council members friendly to HRC (Historical Review Committee) for only the cost of materials. Conning his way seemed his greatest skill. He built a small deck for one of my neighbors and placed the floor boards down the wrong way. Even I know you have to place the "rainbow" of the wood down and not up. It buckled after one snow fall.

One morning around five AM, I heard a loud commotion in the alley. Then I heard Bobby as he stomped around growling. "Gahhh, #?*!" Like Daddy always said, using profanity is a sign of low intelligence.

It was enough to wake the dead. I ran to put my coat on over my night gown and put Pookie's leash on her. I decided to investigate whether or not he needed first aid. As I got out to the back alley I asked him what was wrong. He was so red I could see it by the street light.

"Somebody put marine grease all over my ladders and saw horses. You didn't hear or see anything last night did you?"

I said as quietly as I could- -(considering the hour) "No, what's marine grease? Stuff you put in your hair?"

"Noooo", He said through gritted teeth, you put it on the wheel wells of a boat trailer." He was wiping and wiping his hands. Then he went back in the garage and came out with a roll of paper towels.

"Are you alright then?" I asked.

"Yeah."

Then he began wiping the ladders no thanks or acknowledgement. Charm free that Bobby, not a hint of gratitude for my neighborliness. I wished him luck (which carries no meaning for us Presbyterians) and went back inside. Pookie was jumping up and down from all the excitement. I let her loose in the back yard and waited just long enough for her to tinkle again. Then took her back in and set up the coffee pot. It was so close to the time I usually walked Pookie so I went upstairs and put on my walking clothes. As I put them on I whistled a tune from an ad off of T.V., but it felt like the Hallelujah Chorus. The melody and lyrics were hard to shake in my head. It was an add for free credit scores so I interchanged my words with the free credit score diddy. "Poor Bobby, poor, pitiful, pukey, Bobby." I sang it as I headed downstairs with a spring in my step. There is nothing like seeing a messy, inconsiderate, neighbor get some of what they've been giving.

Most mornings around six, I would be in the alley at my back gate and Bobby would be leaving. So I usually didn't have to speak to him. As I walked my little Pookie, Bobby usually passed me in his truck. His black beast just standing in the truck bed. That particular morning he was too busy cleaning up grease. The incomers ran in the morning around the same time I finished my walk. The Snickelfritz's had a toddler by then and I often saw Vicky and the baby through their kitchen window as I walked by their place. Bert Snickelfritz was always gone. I thought he had awful work hours. At breakfast one morning at the Lick Skillet, I asked Hazel if she still saw them.

"Honey, do I ever! He stops for coffee to go a lot. Bert is always going out of town to play golf."

"I thought he just worked hard."

" He works hard at hardly working. The manager runs the restaurant don't you know."

"Is his Pickle Barrel taking any of your business?"

"Lord no! People out on the highway hadn't ever been my steadies. "Tiggy, I'm a hometown place. 'Sides that, where else can you get the news of the day without buying a paper, huh?"

"Well, what have you heard about Bobby and Darla Tatum?"

"Darla's parents have set her up in a little gift shop uptown. You know her parents have money. I heard they bought the building she's in. Incomers are always coming in here with something from her shop.

But you know Tiggy, Darla always had taste don't you think?"
I nodded affirmatively.

"And why in the name of all that matters did she take up with that Bobby?"

Hazel shook her head. "I think he's some kind of brain washer, or maybe he just put on a good act in order to move up socially. Gosh Tiggy, his people were never church going folks either. Now all of a sudden he's in the choir."

"I see him home nearly every day by three o'clock. He goes running with that horrible dog of his, haven't you seen him run by?" `

"Naw, I'm back figuring my books then. Why do you mention it?"

"Because Hazel, Darla works till after dark, Estelle or Pete take those kids to every lesson under the sun and Bobby gets off early to play. Now just how much help is he?"

"Well, I saw in the paper he was going to help the First Presbyterian build a habitat home over by the All Mart."

He can go in the church every time the door opens as far as I'm concerned Hazel, and it doesn't make him a good person. How you treat your family and neighbors are the real indicator. Not what gets you in the paper!"

"I see what you mean. Did you hear about what Bobby and those incomers are trying to do to Mary Lou Knorr?"

"What do you mean Hazel? Since when is Bobby Tatum any expert on architecture of old homes?"

"He just became an approved contractor on the list the Historical Review Committee has come up with. That historical committee is trying to tell Miss Mary Lou she can't put a new roof on unless it's slate, and her a widow lady without two dimes to rub together!"

"But Hazel, that committee can't tell you what kind of roof to put on."

"Oh yes they can, and what's more, a new slate roof would cost close to thirty thousand dollars! Mr. Loveless over in city planning will fine homeowners that don't comply."

"How can they make any of us put back a roof like the original? It's the person paying the bills who should decide what they want. Or…what they can afford! Anyhoo, why should Dick Loveless help the people who are hurting people he has known all his life?"

She walked over to start the coffee machines, then looked around to see who was near. Then she came over and leaned in to talk.

"The way I understand it, if you already have an asphalt shingle roof and it's historic property you can replace it with asphalt. Bobby said in a letter to the editor, he and Darla can have an asphalt roof only because it's covered under what they call a grandfather clause. If you already have a metal, slate or barrel tile you have to replace the roof with that type no matter what it costs!"

"Well, you just ruined my appetite Hazel. If those yahoos from the Historical Review Committee and Mr. Loveless think they can force a retiree or anybody else for that matter, to make repairs with the most expensive stuff around; then they have got another thing coming to 'em. Furthermore, it's awful funny to me Hazel, that people friendly to the HRC get exceptions made for them!"

"I'm just telling you what Bobby was quoted in the newspaper as saying." "

We'll see about what Bobby can say and what he's gonna be able to get away with!"

As soon as I finished my eggs and last cup of coffee, I made a bee line home to Call Miss Mary Lou.

I dialed the number and waited, she was eighty two and deaf as a post. After what seemed like a hundred rings she answered. "Hello," she said in a shaky voice.

"Miz Mary Lou, this is Tiggy Adams."

"Oh,…..Tiggy, how are you?"

"Fine Miz Knorr, I just heard about your predicament with this so called Review Committee."

"Tiggy, I just don't know what I'm gonna do. I have a leak in my bedroom and one so bad in the kitchen, the plaster is falling in."

"Well Miz Mary Lou, obviously you need a new roof but not a thirty thousand dollar one!"

"Did you hear about that?"

"Yes maam, and the Hill and Dale is going to hear about it too. There must be something we can do if we put our heads together."

"Well, my grandson is going with my son to the next city council meeting to ask for some kind of exception."

I asked her what she was going to do in the meantime. She told me her son and grandson were patching the roof with tar. Then she told me a new asphalt roof would cost five thousand dollars if it weren't for her son. That about knocked the wind out of me too. Then she said her grandson was going to remove her old roof and replace any lumber that needed it. Then the cost would be about three thousand, and she could make payments for that.

"But wouldn't you know Tiggy, I have had a slew of realtors offer to sell my place. They all say they have a buyer for me if I'll list the house with them.

"Baloney sandwich! All those realtors say that. If it's true then why don't they just bring em by to look see and take half their commission?

"Oh......I see what you mean. The thing is Tiggy, I just don't wanna leave this house unless it's feet first."

"I don't blame you Miz Mary Lou, a body oughta be able to stay in their home if they can."

"That's how I feel Tiggy. Besides, my son and grandson do all my grass cutting and what not, which is nice."

"Would they help you with the roof so you wouldn't have to make payments?"

"Oh sure, but they have families to support and I have always paid my own way."

I reminded her that's what family is for. She started rambling about her grandson and I told her I had to go but would be happy to talk to the Review committee. She thanked me and told me she would let me know. We said our goodbyes. The council was due to meet in three days and I was gonna attend that meeting come Hell or High water.

That Sunday, I watched as Darla arrived early to church for choir practice with Bobby in tow. I just rolled my eyes as I looked out the kitchen window of the fellowship hall. I thought next he'll be singing a solo too. That would require fake interest on my part. I didn't trust his new found piety. Estelle came in with Darla and Pete's girls shortly after that. I offered coffee to her. As soon as the girls went upstairs to the Sunday school hall I could talk to her.

"Well, I just saw that Bobby and Darla come to choir practice together." Without meaning to, my expression of disapproval is to refer to something or someone as "that" person, or "that" place.

"Tiggy, he started coming to choir right after he started on Pete and Darla's kitchen. That no good snake is telling anyone who will listen that they met at church and then he was hired to do the kitchen. You know that's a lie from the pits of you know where." Then Estelle pointed to the ground to demonstrate the place she was referring to.

"Estelle, he's just trying to make himself look more respectable."

"Tiggy, he barely opens his mouth, he's so sullen."

"Don't you realize he doesn't know what to say in a social situation. Have you ever heard how his kin folk murder the King's English? Why I bet he doesn't even know what a double negative is. Besides that, he is as ugly as a mud fence."

Estelle said she could tell he was very uneducated and poorly raised. Then we headed up to the sanctuary. When I got home from church, I put on the T.V. while I made myself some lunch. As I surfed the channels, the local public service station reminded me of the City Council meeting that week. I wrote a note to myself on the fridge calendar in red marker. The next morning, as I put the leash on Pookie, I noticed the reminder about the meeting. I told Pookie to make it snappy in doing her business. I had a lot of phone calls to make. I wondered if there would be a lot of incomers at council meeting.

We began our daily walk down our usual route. First, it was out the back door so she could do her business in the alley amongst the underbrush. I refuse to walk around with gray hair and a grocery sack of "doodys". It makes you look like some kind of mental patient. I only carry a plastic bag just in case Pookie happened to go on someone's yard or footpath. The majority of incomers I ran into didn't even have their dogs on a leash. Neither did they make an effort to clean up after them. I was beginning to see "doodys" left on the sidewalk on many a day. It was no different that morning, right there in the middle of the sidewalk was a pile that looked like it came from a small elephant. I was so mad I belted out, "Fudge!"

I tried to find a stick so I could flick it out of the way. It was difficult to see in the minimal light with the sun only halfway up. I was going to bat the pile of fertilizer into the street so nobody would step on it. I saw Lilly Wiley about fifty yards away with Jenny and Beaucoup, (her Welsh Corgis) so I gave her a ten second warning.

"Elephant droppings straight ahead!"

She stopped with a puzzled look. Then she cupped her hands around her mouth so she wouldn't have to yell.

"Tiggy, did you step in a pile of dawg mess?"

"Almost my dear. I'm pitching it into the gutter as we speak." An incomer jogged up silently behind me and nearly scared me out of seven years growth. It, and I couldn't tell you if it was a man or woman, ran around me and my efforts without a word. Next, I picked up Pookie so she wouldn't get into a teedle contest with Jenny and Beaucoup. As Lilly got closer she said, "You can't tell me the owners of that dog didn't know it left a calling card that big!"

"Have you ever heard of anything so inconsiderate in your life?"

Lilly just shook her head, wished me a good day and headed down Main Street.

As I got to the end of the block and turned the corner, another dog confronted Pookie and I. It was a big mongrel that bared it's teeth at us. I grabbed up Pookie and looked around for the owner. I saw an incomer coming down the street about a hundred yards away.

"He won't hurt you."

I've heard that before!" and gave him a look as if he had two heads. The man had a leash in his hand. As he came up to retrieve his dog, I said, "There are leash laws in Mountain Empire you know." He hooked the leash to his dog and took off across the street with his dog in tow. Not an excuse me, or it won't happen again, not boo diddle you squat from the man. I recognized him from the paper as one of the new professors at Mountain Laurel College. His education obviously didn't include manners. Then again, you can't make a silk purse out of a sow's ear. I headed back home the way I came. I didn't want another unpleasant person or animal to deal with.

When I got back home, I picked up the daily paper and unhooked Pookie just inside the front door. I started my coffee pot and settled at the kitchen table to read the paper. The headline that morning was, PRIVATE PROPERTY RIGHTS IN QUESTION. The entire article was about the most recent complaints against the Historical Review Committee. It seemed the neighborhood over by the new elementary school was now the latest target of the "Histrionic" Review Committee. The school was built in 1958 to accommodate all the children born after the Korean War. Even though it wasn't a new school, everybody always referred to it as new.

The neighborhood with the new school was first developed in the twenties. It was called Ivy Heights, with Tudor style homes in the middle of the development. All around it were later built homes. The original developer mismanaged and ran out of money during the depression when around ten bungalows were built. They were nothing fancy, believe me. Ivy Heights wasn't further developed until 1955, the year my daughter was born. Brick ranch homes were thrown up almost overnight in the late fifties and early sixties. It was a convenient neighborhood for families with school age children. My guess was, there were around six Tudors a block in from the entrance and close to thirty brick ranch styles. Three of the Tudors and all of the bungalows had been bought by incomers who were trying to get the entire development designated historic.

I decided to make my first cup of coffee before reading the article, hoping to resurrect a positive morning. I began muttering to myself as I put the sugar in my coffee.

"Who ever heard of a historic brick rancher! Pookie, I just hope your old dog house isn't considered historic. After all, Paw Paw built it for old Jake in 1959. Shhh, we won't mention that to any incomers." I sat down with my coffee and Pookie came over begging for me to pet her. I had gotten her active by talking to her. I shooed her and read on. She went back over to her bed by the refrigerator. It seemed the longstanding citizens were up in arms over the ridiculous idea of making Ivy Heights another historic district like my street. One of the citizens was quoted.

"This neighborhood is a hodge podge of homes-a mix of Tudors, bungalows and ranch styles. These new people are going to pit old against young, rich against poor and we won't stand for it!" Lib's great nephew Brett Wytheville was the feature writer. He lived in the neighborhood too. He stated in the article that the issue of becoming another historical district would divide a friendly neighborhood. Thank Heavens somebody in the Wytheville family cared about this town other than making money off of it. He went on to say that most people agree with preserving older homes as long as the architectural requirements are not too overzealous. He was too kind, telling someone what kind of roof they can put on is beyond the pale of being overzealous. It was downright against the constitution, I just knew it. Big ticket items were just that! A person should be able to do what they could afford. Besides, I thought, who looks at a roof anyway? Only someone with their nose stuck up too high on their big head with little breeding.

From the article I learned there was a president of the Historic Review Committee. He had moved here from Iowa and had attended Mountain Empire Military Academy. He had come through town for a reunion recently and decided to settle here. He now owned one of the bungalows in Ivy Heights. His name was Bill Nibruska and he claimed to have a masters in Historic Preservation. He was quoted in the article.

"These guidelines are in place through Mountain Empire City Council and they are solely to protect property values. Residents of Sherwood Ave area and any other new designees must apply for certificates of appropriateness when considering any work to be done on their house. Each proposed change or maintenance must be accompanied by a fifty dollar application fee. Then, they will be reviewed and voted on by the Historical Review Committee to ensure nothing conflicts with the period in which the home was built."

I remembered seeing this Mr. Nibruska somewhere recently, but couldn't put my finger on it. He had the coldest eyes, like there was nothing behind them.

Brett asked him in the article just what work required a certificate. The list was as long as your arm. They were as follows:
Paint Colors
New Construction

Alterations or additions
Demolitions(partial or complete)
Reconstruction or relocation
Changes to windows or doors
Changes to siding or roof materials
Changes to walls or fences
New signage

I thought to myself, this Bill Nibruska is all wrapped up in himself and his power. You know the old saying, A man wrapped up in himself, makes a very small package. I decided to run my errands early so I could take time to dress up a bit for the city council meeting that evening. It promised to be an interesting one. This evening was going to be like the weather report, it wasn't going to please everybody. I called Estelle to see if she had read the front page but she wasn't home. Then I called Lilly. I asked her about the article in the paper. She was in a state of shock over it.

"Tiggy, did you know there were so many rules and regulations with that Historical mess?"

"No I did not, nor did I ever imagine any place in the United States Of America could tell you what you can and cannot do to your own home and charge you fifty dollars to be told yes or no!"

"Well, Tiggy do you realize if I replace my upstairs windows with the ones you don't have to paint, they could stop me?" "Lilly, I say, go on and do what you want and say nothing." "That's an idea. But how can you keep a secret like that in this town? I kept my bathroom light on one night by accident and three people asked me the next day if I had been sick!

3 TAKING COUNCIL

I dressed for success before going to the city council meeting that night. My hair had been in a bob all my life, but the latest look my beautician gave me was stacked. Everyone in the Hill and Dale said with my size four figure and young looking skin, I should dye my hair. Lilly and Estelle kept trying to talk me into coloring over the large white chunks at the front but I was way past fooling with that. Just give me my Lilac Champagne lipstick to bring out my eyes and a little eyebrow pencil and I can take the town. I put on my best designer pantsuit. It was a soft blue-gray which is one of my best colors. Lilly Wiley backed out on going with me at the last minute. Her flimsy excuse was she no longer went out after dark. I had a problem parking which I hoped was a good sign. The more townspeople that attended the better I say.

As I came in city hall I ran into Woody, he made a point to speak to me.

"Tiggy, how are you? What brings you to this meeting?" "I'm here to see about all this stuff with the Historical Review Committee." He blanched slightly.

"It's all about progress Tiggy, that's all."

"I couldn't agree more Woody, and I mean Miss Mary Lou making progress on having a roof she can afford!"

He held the elevator door for me and some young people I didn't recognize. He smiled and greeted them as if he knew them. Then one of them said, "Mr. Green, I brought the drawings of that pergola we want on the front."

Woody smiled and said "Mighty fine." I'd just bet they had hired him or his sons to build it. No doubt their plans would be approved.

I parted ways with Woody as we entered the room filled with folding chairs. All eight members of the council were seated facing us at a table up front. That Bill Nibruska, head of the HRC was on the tail end of the right side of the table. Nobody and I mean nobody, but the minister whose turn it was to open the meeting, ever sat with council. I started to sit somewhere in the middle and then thought better of it. I grabbed the closest aisle seat to the front as possible. I was in a sea of incomers, with their Jesus sandals, no makeup and dressed for yard work if you ask me. The meeting was called to order. I looked around for people I knew. The entire Knorr family was seated on the other side of the aisle from me. There was Miss Mary Lou, her son, two grandsons and a few of her neighbors. Bobby Tatum and Carter Crawford came in as the minutes from the previous month were read. Then it dawned on me, no one had opened the meeting with prayer and the pledge of Allegiance. Our mayor, Lamarr Hunt, said in a cautious tone, "Is there any new business?"

Some foreigner stood up and spoke in very broken English. "Hallo, I am Krishna Dipendrah." (He pronounced it, Creesh-nah Depend-rah) "I would like to request you allow me to purchase beelding next to my beeziness for making convenient store." I suppose he meant to say convenience store. "Theese store weel need to have wall removed in order to be connected to office of gas station."

Then Lamarr turned to that Nibruska man.

"Bill I believe it's you that oughta address Mr. Dapendra's request."

"In light of the fact your gas station is in the historic district of the West Beverley area, we must first have a set of plans to view. Those plans must be in accordance with the structures on either side of you."

"Ah, and if I bring deez plans to you before next meeting you can tell me yes at ofeeshal meeting?"

Nibruska paused and said, "You may bring your plans to the office next door to the city planner's office with a check for fifty dollars any time before the next meeting."

"Thank you veddy much." Then he sat down.

In the past, anybody, even a foreigner, could have bought that uptown property and made it into anything God fearing people would go to. But now it was all about the money for applying, and then using who the HRC approved of. Somehow, money was going into someone's pocket.

Before another word could be uttered, Jimmy Knorr and his mother stood up. Lamarr recognized them to speak.

"Good evening council, I am here on behalf of my elderly mother."

Well, I thought.....do you have to use the word old? But if sympathy and respect for the elderly works........

Jimmy continued, "I have in my hands a letter from Bill Nibruska telling my mother, who can barely afford to live on a fixed income, she cannot have an asphalt roof installed. Sir, protecting the look of historic homes is a fine idea; however, a new roof is the most obvious way to *preserve* her 1895 era home." Nibruska tried to get Lamarr's attention but Jimmy continued uninterrupted.

"A new roof of the original slate will cost more than Mama's yearly income. I am requesting here, and in the letter Mama brought for a variance due to financial hardship." Lamarr started to defer that to Nibruska and Jimmy said,

"Lamarr, I have known you all my life and I would like you to answer." Lamarr turned red as a beet.

"It is up to the city council Jimmy but the covenants of the Historical Review board are now a prerequisite to construction and improvements in your Mama's neighborhood."

"If I may," Nibruska said, "The style of your mother's house requires either a slate roof like the original or a variance for a metal roof, also appropriate to the Queen Anne Style of her house."

Miss Mary Lou stood up and said, "A metal roof would cost me fifteen thousand, two thousand more than my yearly income, are you willing to pay the difference over what I can afford?"

Her son added, "Mama's house may be in the Queen Anne style, but Mama does not have a retirement check fit for a queen!" Well, that brought a giggle. All the men at the table looked as if they were playing stump the monkey. They all looked at each other, shuffled papers and began making hand signals at each other, trying to get someone to take the hot seat.

I stood up and said, "There's no sense in y'all sitting up there like a mime troupe, Miss Mary Lou has a legitimate request. Either the Historical Review Committee pays the difference for the roof they want or they are just plain discriminating against the poor and elderly!" Then I directed a question at Nibrushka. "What's it gonna be *Mr. Ni-brusk*?"

"It's Nibruska." He said

I smiled through my teeth and said, "Pardon me, you may continue."

"Thank you. Folks, I know it's hard to adjust to new rules but they were voted on and duly passed by council." Someone shouted from the back,

"It wasn't explained to the town just how the Review Committee would be in the business of trouncing private property rights!"

I stood up and asked, "Which *man* (and I meant the term loosely) is going to answer the question about who pays?" Jimmy Jr. stood up on the other side of his Daddy, "Yeah!"

Lamarr turned his mike up and cleared his throat, "Please everybody sit down. We will entertain a variance for an asphalt shingle roof at the next meeting."

Jimmy stood up but his mother spoke first, "Lamarr, I have new leaks popping up every time it rains. I have got to do something yesterday!" Mr. Krishna Dipendrah sat through all of the discourse staring straight ahead, still as a corpse. You couldn't even tell if he was breathing.

Lamarr said, "Jimmy just bring in your variance request," Jimmy interrupted, "Lamarr, anyone can make part of the minutes an official request, so consider Mama's letter here as the second official request." Then he took a piece of paper from Mary Lou and walked up to the table and gave it to Lamarr. Then he said thank you to Lamarr and went back to where his family was and ushered them out. I said loud enough for everybody to hear, "They still didn't answer the question." Nobody from the head table would look at me. The next order of business was from an incomer with a request to put a pergola over his front porch. It seemed to have already been decided before the meeting. Bill Nibruska took his drawing of the proposal, his fifty dollar check and looked it over for a few seconds. Then he told Dick Loveless from city planning he didn't see a problem. I stood up to be recognized just as the incomer sat down after his obviously pre-approved pergola request.

"I would like to have a public accounting of projects approved by the Historical Review Committee and council that benefit any members financially." You could have heard a pin drop. The head table began looking like a mime troupe again. I stood there, not about to sit down.

Finally, one of the members leaned into his mike and said, "We'll do our best Tiggy."

"Just give the newspaper the list or post it by the assessor's office." Then I sat down thinking surely the local paper would jump on finally reporting something newsworthy.

Next, the school board business started and before long the meeting was adjourned. I got on the elevator with incomers and Mountain Empire citizens. One of the citizens said, "You had a good point about who's bank account benefits from all these new historical rules."

I looked around at the incomers as if to say, hit me with your best shot. "I intend to find out if we have a new boy network to replace the old boy network. Since the new boy network isn't even from around here, they can just get back in their car and take the Histerical Review Committee with them."

The man just laughed and said, "You got that right Miz Adams." The incomers all looked at their feet and imaginary dust on the ceiling. As I got to my car it started to rain. Poor Miss Mary Lou, I had visions of her putting pots all around to catch leaks. It rained hard all night and I didn't sleep well, thinking of how overreaching that Historical Review Committee was.

The next morning it was still overcast so I turned on the local channel for the weather report. The report that day was for overcast with only a slight chance of rain. How prophetic, I thought to myself, it is a dark day when your town is suddenly overrun by incomers with no interest in preserving anything but the architecture with drafty old windows. I hurried to put the leash on Pookie and we headed out the back door to the alley. I noticed I had forgotten to lock the sliding door by the breakfast table, so I locked it. Pookie and I headed down the alley when I sensed someone behind me. I turned to see that monster of Bobby Tatum's. Pookie started barking like she had a barking tape in her brain.

"Get back Gus!" I grabbed up Pookie, still barking her head off.

Bobby came out of nowhere. "Gus! No!". The monster retreated and I turned on my heels, not about to wait for an apology that would never come. I put Pookie down and we started out of the alley after she did her business. I kept my eyes peeled behind me for any more disturbance. I was ready to kick that dog into next year if he came after us again.

As I walked past all the houses I took note of how none of the incomers ever hung curtains. They may call that light and airy on the decorator shows but I call it exhibitionism in my book. I decided to walk a little farther than our usual square block so I could see if Miss Mary Lou was up. Her lights were on in the kitchen. Just as I approached her front, her grandson drove up with some young men I didn't know. I don't think he recognized me because he didn't speak. Next, a truck from a roofing company drove up and parked on the yard. I wouldn't have stood for that after the rain we had the night before, it tears up a yard. I kept on past the house and saw no less than five incomers running. I passed two more incomers on bicycles dressed in helmets with chin straps, glow in the dark pants and leather gloves. For crying out loud, they looked like a bunch of crash test dummies. Then who should run by but that Bill Nibruska. One of the incomers stopped him and asked him if he was pleased with the new central air. It was only late April, nobody even used a fan until mid-May. I stopped to give Pookie a rest, so I overheard Nibruska bragging about having all of his floors sanded.

Then the other man asked him if he was going to stay in the house when the varnish was applied. He said he planned to leave the windows open until the smell abated. "Well, when does the refinishing start?" the incomer asked Nibruska.

"Day after tomorrow." He said.

Pookie and I walked on and just as I reached Lib's, she walked out on her front porch and motioned to me frantically.

I got to her first step and she began spitting her words. "Tiggy, I want you to come and see what has happened to my hedge!" She led me up one side of it and down the other. "Do you see what I see?" she said. There were at least a half dozen yellow and brown patches.

"Lib, that is from a dog urinating!"

"Don't I know it! And I know this much: it's a big black dog that's doing it. I've seen it once or twice. I have also found large poo piles in my front."

"Well Lib, I know of one big, black, dog that runs loose every morning around five. It's Bobby Tatum's."

"What am I going to do Tiggy, we have never had dogs running loose like that." I promised her I would start getting up earlier to see if I could catch the monster.

"I'll get one of those throw away cameras; Lib and you do the same. That way we can prove whose dog is responsible." I headed for home, returning through the front door as usual so I could get my paper. I headed back to the kitchen and started my coffee. The paper was full of the business before city council concerning Miss Mary Lou's roof.

There was no mention of my request concerning who had benefited financially on the council. Following the money was the most effective way to stop all this nonsense. There was constant work being done on the incomer homes. The phone rang and it was Lilly.

"Tiggy, you didn't get out in all that rain last night did you?"

"Lilly, it rained as I was leaving the meeting. You should have been there to stick up for Miss Mary Lou."

"Tiggy, I know you said things better than I ever could." "Well thank you for your vote of confidence, I just want these incomers to know their place."

Then I told her about my run in with Bobby's dog and Lib's boxwoods.

"Oh Lib must be so upset! Those boxwoods are English. If you prune away the yellow places it could take years for them to fill back out, and you know how she is about them."

I tried for a week to catch Bobby's dog running loose but without success. At the end of the week, there was too much excitement to worry about Lib's boxwoods. It turned out the people I saw in front of Miss Mary Lou's removed her slate roof and put a brand new asphalt shingle one on. Dick Loveless slapped a zoning lien on her property for the cost of a new slate roof and all hell broke loose. In the same week, Bill Nibruska's house burned to the ground and he and his wife barely made it out alive. The article in the paper about the fire was interesting to me. Brett Wytheville interviewed him. According to the paper, Bill got back from running one morning and found two fans on his back stoop with a note attached. It read, "thought you could use these while your varnish dries".

He used the fans for a couple of days, and in the middle of the night they were awakened by the smell of smoke. The fans had shorted out or something. The fire chief was interviewed in the article and explained what happened. "The fans responsible for the fire at 280 Ivy Glen were SMC brand oscillating floor fans. The electric cord can be damaged by the oscillation motion. Damage to the cord can result in a short circuit and ignition of the plastic casing poses the fire hazard. Now, that fan has not been sold for some time, it was recalled two years ago. I have spoken to the manufacturer and verified the model number was distributed three years ago to several home improvement chains in Florida, Virginia, Tennessee and North Carolina. The company placed the recall notice over through the news media two years ago. The recall was well publicized." According to the paper, although everybody and their brother knew about his floors being redone, no one had stepped up to the plate to acknowledge they had loaned the fans. I can understand that, who wants to be killed for kindness?

After reading the article I called Lilly. "Have you read the morning paper?"

"Can you believe it Tiggy? Miss Mary Lou having a lien put on her house by the city for fixing her leaky roof!"

"Lilly, how about the article about the fire at Bill Nibruska's house."

"Oh that. I'm still digesting what they did to poor Mary Lou. Her son told me the night of their meeting with city council she came home to more leaks than she had pans to catch. Jimmy said there was no way he was going to wait a month for permission to fix his mama's roof. He figured nobody would dare go after an old lady like that."

I said emphatically, "Lilly, you would be surprised how Woody and all those councilmen coddle that Historical Review Committee. They have more power than I gave them credit for." "Tiggy, you know what my Walter used to say about politicians and folks like that?"

"No, but I know you'll tell me." "Walter said, "Some folks in government have more power than a bad person should have or a good person should want."

"Did he make that up Lilly? That is the most profound thing I think I ever heard."

"No Tiggy, he didn't think it up, but you know he read the Reader's Digest from cover to cover every month. He probably got it out of that."

"Well, I'm going to use that Lilly. I don't know when or where, but I'm gonna use it." A few minutes later, we said our goodbyes and I went back to reading my paper. The editorials were all about Mary Lou's predicament. I was right in the middle of one when the phone rang. It was Estelle Gwaltney, she sounded hopped up she was so excited.

"Tiggy, Jimmy Knorr is asking everyone to put a sign on their car and in their front yard!" She took a breath loudly enough for me to think she was smoking something. Before I could get out the words, "What kind of sign?" she began elaborating. "The sign should say : Remove the lien off Mary Lou, she's our friend and she's eighty two."

Well, I just howled over that, it could have tickled me to next week.

Estelle said sheepishly, "I thought up the rhyme, I thought you of all people were sympathetic to her."

"Oh Estelle I am, I AM! I will be out to put my sign up with bells on. I'll take one of those cardboard inserts in a new pantyhose and make another for the side window of my car."

"Well, that's more like it."

"Estelle, you know I will do everything in my power to stop these Historical Nazis. You know who is really responsible, it's that Hugh McMinn. He's the one who started the whole Review Committee. It's Hugh that paid that lawyer from Washington to help them go through all the steps the city requires to be able to do things like they're doing to Mary Lou. I wish Hugh's house had burned down too."

"Now Tiggy, I know you don't mean that."

"Well, I would settle for someone to break his leg. Is that better?"

"You are awful!"

"No, it's these incomers pushing their agenda of greed that are awful. Seriously though, my resentment is personal, not active. So, I take back what I said about wishing anybody harm. In the long run, it all comes out in the wash."

Then I told her good bye. She gave her signature hang up by spelling "B, Y".

I called Carter Crawford and left a message on his answering machine to call me. I was going to need a man to fix me a sturdy sign and hammer it in my front yard. I went upstairs to look for a new package of pantyhose. I found one and took out the little cardboard mould that the stockings were wrapped around. In my kitchen drawer I found a permanent marker used for marking leftovers. In all capital letters I wrote Estelle's little diddy. TAKE THE LIEN OFF MARY LOU, SHE'S OUR NEIGHBOR AND SHE'S NINETY TWO!!!!!!!!! I got my roll of masking tape from the same drawer as the pen and put the sign and tape by my purse so I wouldn't forget.

I cleaned up the kitchen and headed upstairs to dress for the day. I was almost out of everything so it was going to be the grocery store first today. It could be a good thing if that Mr. Krishna could open a little grocery place like we used to have uptown. Then I would't have to shop at the All Mart. Hugh McMinn had opened a truck wash right at the top of where the state road intersected the town road. You wouldn't catch me traveling that way after dark. There was only a stop sign at the end of the town road. There had consistently been wrecks right as you turn off town road even before the big semis began using the truck wash. I don't know how many times people asked council to put a traffic light at the very spot. The answer was always it costs too much. Another legitimate reason for me not wanting to shop at the All Mart was the rude people. Unless I went in there before eight am, it was too crowded for my taste. The strangers who came off the highway and all the county folks took all the good parking. There have been times where I have been in the store, said excuse me or pardon me, (in order to get down the aisle) and the people I was speaking to just looked at me. Worse yet, didn't even acknowledge my presence. Somebody needs to bring back etiquette and I don't mean maybe!

While in the All Mart I ran into Carter. For a minute I thought he saw me and went the other way.

"Carter," I said forcefully.

He stopped and spoke to me, asked me how I was, sort of sheepishly. I asked him if he had gotten my message about needing some carpentry help.

"This wouldn't be about those signs I heard folks are gonna be putting up about Miz Knorr would it? I answered in the affirmative and he rolled his eyes.

"Is there a problem old friend?" I said as I batted my eyes. "Well, you see, uh, Miz Tiggy, I just don't wanna be a part of any hard feelings."

"Carter Allan Crawford, I have known you all your life. How could you have any feelings but sympathy and loyalty for Mary Lou?"

"It's just, well,................ the new folks gives me a lot of business. I can see both sides, it's all legal what the history people are doing."

"Well, if you lived in our neck of the woods you wouldn't want anyone telling you what to do with your property! Your home that's bought and paid for by you!"

He told me he understood how we felt but he didn't want anyone seeing him putting any signs up. I didn't want to lose him as my helper. I could have remarried several times but the only men I needed in my life were a good mechanic, a decent plumber and someone to do odd jobs. It gave me pause to think about alienating him.

"I'll tell you what Carter, you just make me a two foot by two foot sign, spray it white and bring it over after dark. How's that from one old friend to another?" Then I pierced him with my former Miss Mountain Empire smile. He chuckled and assured me he would bring it by that night.

The lunch special that day at the Lick Skillet was meat loaf and the latest on the fire and Mary Lou. I went for a BLT and all that Hazel knew. The first thing she noticed was the sign on my right rear window.

"Tiggy, did you come up with that idea?" I informed her it was straight from Jimmy by way of Estelle. There were incomers in the café but Hazel is one of us through and through.

"I need me one of those signs." She then smiled at an incomer and offered them more sweet tea. "Are you going to the council meeting this week?" she asked me.

"I wouldn't miss it for all the tea in China." I said proudly.

Then we talked about poor Mr. Nibruska, having to stay out by the highway in a hotel until he could do something about a place to live. I had details for Hazel on how poor Mr. Krishna was trying to turn the building next to the gas station into a convenience store. We both agreed there needed to be somewhere you could go to get essentials without going to the All Mart. Hazel listened with amazing concentration as I recounted all that had happened at the previous city council meeting. She could flip a hamburger, pour coffee and hand someone the ketchup without ever taking her eyes off of you. She leaned close. "Nibruska is awful full of himself. Hugh McMinn is the power behind him, trust me on that."

"What do you know about those two Hazel?"

"That's the thing, they and their wives are guarded as anything about what they did before they moved here. You have to wonder why these incomers had no roots anywhere. The couple that bought across from Lib have never even been in here."

"You mean the ones who bought the Johnson restaurant Hazel?" "Naw, I mean the other ones from New York, the artists."

I had forgotten about them since it was rare to see the two of them. All the other incomers were childless except for them and the Snickelfritzes. Children bring you out in the yard. Well, at least the mothers socialize. Mrs. "Pookay"/Puckett wasn't in anything at the school or any church. They were both four square for the Historical Review Committee and that was all I needed to know.

"It's not unusual that you never see them, they only socialize with incomers and particularly those on the Review Committee."

Just then someone came up to the register to pay their check. Then an incomer came to the register. I knew he had seen me drive up with my car sign. I smiled my best smile and he said hello, as he smiled sardonically. I shot back a "kiss my foot" smile and then turned on the ice with a "What are you doing on my earth?" look. Hazel told everybody to have a nice day no matter what. I finished up lunch and headed home.

That evening I was watching the local news when I heard a knock on the sliding door. I looked up and saw Carter Crawford. I let him in at the back door right by the sliding one.

"I knocked on the other door but the T.V. drowned it out." "Oh, maybe I'm getting a little hard of hearing." I said. He had the sign I wanted. I asked him what I owed him. I went to my purse to get the eight dollars.

"Remember now, you didn't get this from me."

I told him to think nothing of it and bid him good night. I went down to the laundry shelf in the basement, looking for my big hammer. It was on the utility shelf on the other side of the room.

"Gotcha."

Next I laid the sign on the floor, grabbed the black spray paint I used on the porch chairs every year. With purpose I sprayed the slogan on. It dripped a little but it was still legible, perfectly legible. Out to the front yard I went. I turned on my porch light so I could see. I looked down the block and saw no less than five signs. I proudly and forcefully began hammering my sign in.

An incomer jogged by and barely took notice. Bobby Tatum rode by on his racing bike, dressed like the incomers. He looked like a crash test dummy too. I ignored him as best I could. Darla was standing on the sidewalk, so I waved at her and she waved back very nonchalantly. It was nice enough to sit out now, just warm enough without shirt sleeves. I knew why she was out with Bobby. If I had taken up with my married handy man I'd watch him closely too. What anybody as attractive as Darla saw in that runt, I'll never know. When I went back inside, the phone was ringing. It was Estelle calling to find out if I had put my sign up. I didn't betray a trust, so I left out the fact Carter had made it for me. He apparently made hers too because she told me the person who made hers wished to remain anonymous. "Then let's just leave it at that." I told her. Estelle went into detail about the clothes she had just bought for her granddaughters. They were going with Darla to Memphis to see their other grandparents as soon as school let out.

I asked her how long they would be gone and she said two weeks. I didn't want to make her worry, but I saw them come home to an empty house every day. The girls would take the key from the planter, open the back door and disappear inside until their Daddy came to take them to piano or dancing. It would have concerned Estelle to hear they no longer played outside after school.

"Law Estelle, where has this year gone?"

"The last two months have felt like a year, hadn't they?" We both agreed on that.

I remembered about Lib's boxwoods and begged off the phone so I could get to bed early. "B,Y," Estelle said and I headed upstairs.

The next morning I jumped out of bed like I'd been shot out of a cannon. I was on a mission to save my friend's ancient boxwoods. Pookie watched me like she was watching a tennis match. This time I set up the coffee maker so I would come back to the aroma. Pookie and I slipped out the back door and headed toward East Beverley. Pookie kept stopping to smell.

"Come on girl!" I chided quietly.

She looked up at as if to say, "I usually don't get out this early, so I've got to see if there are any new smells." We hit our stride after she did her business and headed up Lib's block. All of a sudden this huge, dark mass of fur was running towards us. It nearly caused me to fall. I grabbed Pookie.

"Get away dog!" I kicked at the air and raised my arm. The dog ran back in the direction it had come from, Lib's end of the block. I followed on the sidewalk holding Pookie close. She barked like she was now as tall as me. "Shush up girl" I said. I reached Lib's and there he was-that monster of Bobby's! He was hiking his leg right on the boxwoods. Bobby came running up behind me in skimpy shorts. I stood my ground.

"Bobby, I know you are new to town living. Did you know there is a leash law?"

He stopped and ran in place as he called the dog. "Gus! Come here!" The dog cowered over to him. I told him his dog had just baptized Lib Shelby's boxwoods. He told me he would try to keep the dog on the other side of the street. Now I ask you, is that an answer? Then he smiled a silly grin and took off running with the dog in tow. No apology, no resolution, not diddley squat! Lib's husband's grandmother planted the boxwoods in 1903, the year the house was built. They were Lib's pride and joy just as Jenny and Beaucoup were to Lilly. The whole town looked forward to Lib's Christmas lights all swagged down the whole length of the hedge.

I called Lib as soon as I could get in the back door. I didn't go through the front like usual. The thought of even seeing that Bobby, twice in one morning, was two times too many. Lib said she watched out the window as I confronted Bobby. I asked her why she didn't come out and tell him to keep his dog off her property.

"I thought you were going to take a picture." She said. Then I realized in my haste to get going I had forgotten the camera.

"O.K. Lib, here's what we do. You keep the camera by the front door. That way you can just stand inside the screen to use the camera. Only remember to press that flash thing-a-ma-jig before snapping the picture."

I gave her my word I would put my camera by Pookie's leash. That way I was sure to remember it. We had a plan we could stick to. Before I could get a picture of Gus desecrating Lib's hedge, Bobby wasn't able to do anything but let the dog out in the fenced back yard. The day after school let out for the year, Darla had left with the children and Bobby had a fall. According to Hazel, he came back from running one morning and slipped on the rug at the back door. He had to crawl to the phone to call for help. When his hired help came to rescue him, he slipped too. Fortunately, he caught himself before hitting the floor.

"Hazel, that is just a shame."

She then told me that Bobby's employee told her the cleaning lady had mistaken car wax for floor wax. She had used it on the floor by mistake. Come to think of it, the bottles are both plastic and yellowish. It was a mistake anyone could make. Hazel told me she heard the car wax was in greatest concentration under the floor mat.

"He had to have the whole entry hall professionally cleaned to make sure the slickness was gone, according to Hazel."

I thought to myself Lib's boxwoods have a reprieve for now. It made sense now as to why I hadn't been able to catch Bobby and his dog. Lib said Bobby had a broken shoulder, wrist and a torn knee.

"Goodness gracious- -Poor thing, that Bobby!"

4 DOG DAYS

The Sunday after hearing about Bobby's accident, I noticed several cars in each church parking lot with Mary Lou signs. Bobby didn't show up at church that day. With Darla still in Memphis and his incapacitation, it was no wonder. After church, Lib, Lilly, Estelle and I decided to lunch at the Johnson. Lilly was having a problem with her windows just like poor Mary Lou had with her roof. She said she had Carter caulk and caulk, but rain still leaked in.

"I've had Carter price new ones. To have what the Historical Committee approves of will cost close to five hundred dollars a window, installed."

Lib asked, "What are they made of, pure gold?"

"No, but they are supposed to be all wood and the same trimmings as the old."

I asked her what the cheaper windows would cost and she said about two hundred installed. We ended up asking in chorus,

"What is wrong with putting those windows from Home Improvement Warehouse, they look just like the old?"

"Search me what all the fuss is about. Not only do those windows have a permanent finish, they save you money. What the Historical people are trying to make me do will be more costly, I just don't like it. I was told I cannot repaint my house colonial blue again because my house is a Prairie style."

I said, "Lib, couldn't Shelby talk to these people and get them to back off?"

"I love Shelby, but she has never listened to me or anybody else for that matter."

I asked Estelle what colors she had to choose from for this so called "Prairie" style.

"I can have several shades of green, brown, baby poo brown or gold.

"That is ridiculous Stelle." Lilly said.

I agreed. "Your favorite color is blue and Colonial blue has always looked fine on your house."

Estelle said she had thought of putting siding on the house so she would not have to paint again. She looked at all of us, "You can forget that. I was told no home in the historic area can ever have siding."

As we finished and walked each other out to the parking lot I prophesied. "We are going to come up with an antidote to the Historical Review Committee, count on it!"

That evening I called Lib because I didn't get a chance to discuss her boxwood problem at lunch. She said that there were new patches of yellow on her boxwoods. I told her I knew Bobby Tatum wasn't able to get around yet. I asked her if she had seen the animal who did it. "I just keep sleeping until seven and seem to miss whoever is doing it.

"Lib, it's time to take this nuisance to the city council. I'm going to the meeting tomorrow night to see that Mary Lou is vindicated from all this persecution she's been under."

"Tiggy, if I thought it would do any good I'd go. Fact is, there is already a leash law. What else can be done? You can't make people behave. You can't legislate consideration!"

"That's a bunch of fertilizer, Lib; we've got laws against murder, stealing, trespassing, don't tell me nothing can be done to enforce leash laws too."

"Well, will you drive Tiggy?"

"Absolutely. Pick you up around six-thirty?"

"That'd be fine.

"Oh and Lib, in the meantime, take as many pictures as you can of the damage to your hedge. I'll get out the pictures from Mattie Fisher's wake. I have your front hedge from several angles." Lib left us that day, resigned to the fact she was gonna have to get tough about this thing. She needed to think like a man!

It was almost time for my favorite Sunday night mystery on PBS. I went upstairs to get in my pajamas and robe when I remembered Pookie needed one more time out in the yard. As I picked up the leash she nearly jumped herself silly she was so excited to go out. We went out the back door and I noticed someone through the break in the fence boards. I couldn't tell if it was a man or woman. Pookie began to pull towards the back gate, barking. I didn't think anything about it. I knew Darla's kids were back so it might have been one of them. There was a slight breeze and it felt good. I would be fine with the windows open and no fan tonight. Before I got back in the door, I heard a horrible commotion coming from the front. I closed the door fast, left Pookie standing in the kitchen with her leash on and headed to the front door.

Lilly was coming up my walkway, her shin bleeding like a stuck pig. Beaucoup's right shoulder, close to his neck was squirting blood.

"Oh my garden peas! Sit right down and I'll get some bandages. Then I'll bring the car around and we'll go to the vet!" I ran to the kitchen.

Lilly hollered through the front screen, "Beaucoup needs a tourniquet!" I grabbed an old tablecloth out of the dining room sideboard and ran back to the front. We tied it where Beaucoup was bleeding. Then I ran back inside for a clean dish cloth for Lilly's leg. I hustled back to the phone in the entry hall. I couldn't find the phone book. I found it in the kitchen and called the vet. I got an answering machine with forty leven options. I left a message and then called our family doctor. He had retired but he could stitch up Beaucoup as good as anyone. Doc Wiley, (Lilly's late husband's cousin) answered and told us to come around to his work shed in the back yard.

I hollered down the hall to tell Lilly I was getting ready to pull the car around. I stopped long enough to take the leash off

Pookie, then flew out the door ninety to nothing. It took both of us to get Beaucoup in the car. He was weak and breathing hard from stress. I didn't bother to fasten a seatbelt. We headed for Ivy Heights. It was only five blocks away, but they were long ones. I passed the former site of Mr. Nibruska's house, a block into Ivy Glen Rd. There didn't look like enough wood left from that house to make a tooth pick. Ivy Heights looked like a war zone, with every other house under some kind of renovation. There were rent-a-dumpsters everywhere, filled to the brim with old kitchen cabinets and debris. Doc Wiley motioned us around his old Tudor to the shed behind his garage. He had already made a soft place on a table for Beaucoup. He gave Beaucoup a shot that the dog didn't even register. Then he stitched him up just as pretty as a picture. As he was finishing and cleaning up the dog's leg he asked Lilly to let him look at hers.

"Lilly, you are going to need a few stitches too." He went into a cabinet and brought out more equipment. Doc cleaned her leg and gave her a shot.

"Ahhrgh!", came from Lilly.

"Lilly, count backwards from ten." Then he began stitching her up.

"Can you feel that?"

"Not really Oscar, it doesn't hurt if that's what you're asking."

He then asked her how it had all happened. I had heard snippets on our ride over in the car but I was too upset to add anything.

"Well, we were just on the last round of our walk, when out of nowhere this great big ole dog, it was black and brown, came running up to us. First he wagged his tail, then he sniffed Beaucoup and suddenly attacked Beaucoup for no reason! I tried to push it off Beaucoup and that's when it bit down on my leg." Doc asked, "Did you recognize the dog?"

"No Oscar, I've never laid eyes on it."

"Well, it is going to have to be identified and quarantined to make sure there's no chance it has rabies."

Doc, it's a shame it has taken bodily harm to finally do something about these people letting their dogs run loose."

Oscar told us he was having the same problem in Ivy Heights.

"I'll bet it wasn't a problem til all these incomers moved here."

Doc smiled, "I see you're familiar with our problems in Ivy Heights."

"That's because we have the same problems in the Sherwood area. And those problems are called incomers."

Doc helped Lilly and Beaucoup to my car. I had left Jenny in the car with the windows all halfway down. I would have brought her out if it had been hotter. Jenny had slobbered a big stain on the inside of every window. As we headed home, Lilly suddenly remembered Jenny and Beaucoup were supposed to be in the dog show up in Salem, Virginia the end of the month.

"I better let Ronnie and Sandy know about what happened." Ronnie and Sandy were the two men who owned and ran the doggie beauty parlor. It was called: CANINE COIFFURES. Ronnie and Sandy also directed weddings and set up receptions on the side. They have been roommates since they graduated from Vo-

Tech as veterinary assistants. Ronnie and Sandy can sure put on a good party. They pay their taxes and they wear matching, turquoise rings. That's all I'm gonna say.

Next morning, I was so unnerved about Lilly and Beaucoup, I was scared to go out with Pookie. I took her out in my robe for a tinkle and came in to dress in walking clothes. I thought the better of being prisoner in my own home and set out with her anyway. I kept a close eye around for the new monster. Darla was out with Bobby's dog and it was on a leash, thank you very much. The early morning crowd of crash test dummies on parade was out in full force. It wasn't until I got around to the front of my block I noticed a strange car in front of Hugh and Betty McMinn's. The car had a Richmond tag, so I guessed their daughter was in for a visit.

No sooner had I passed the car when a young woman came bounding out with a big brown and black dog. It was a "Spicca", my word for an ASPCA dog. Pookie was a "Spicca" too. I grabbed up Pookie quick as a wink and of course the barking tape went off in her head. The young woman did not have the dog on a leash. "How do you do? Is that your dog?"

She said yes in a cautious tone.

"Was the dog out last night around sevenish?"

"Who wants to know?"

I smiled a smile the nurse gives you before she gives you a shot.

"I'm your next door neighbor. My best friend was attacked last night. She tried to stop a dog fitting the description of yours from hurting her dog. She said the dog was black and brown. The doctor that stitched up my friend and her Welsh Corgi will need to speak to you. If Lilly identifies the dog as yours......" I didn't get to finish my sentence.

"My dog wouldn't hurt a fly."

"Then you will understand why your dog must be eliminated as a suspect."

"Fine."

Then she caught the dog by the collar and went inside Hugh and Betty's. I had no sooner gotten in the front door, when I called the police and told them about Lilly. They agreed to come right over and photograph the dog until Lilly could identify it.

I had forgotten to get my paper so I went back to the front porch to get it. Wouldn't you know, Hugh and Betty were hurriedly loading a basket of laundry and other stuff into the girl's car. Betty had the dog on a leash and Hugh looked like a thunder cloud.

"Come on Susan, get a move on!"

I grabbed my camera and walked close enough to get a picture of the dog. I got it just before they noticed me. Hugh turned red as a tomato and looked away. I marched into the house and called the police. They were on their way. They must have driven up as the McMinn girl drove away. No sooner had I called the non-emergency number at the police station to tell them I had a picture of the dog Susan McMinn was wisking away when the patrolmen knocked on my door. As I began relating what had happened the night before, one of them had me start over while he wrote it down. I gave them Lilly's address and they headed over to her house. I called to tell her they were on their way but before I could give her the details about that Susan McMinn, she had to answer the door. She forgot we hadn't rung off and left the phone on the table by the door while she talked to the police. I went ahead and hung my phone up. It would have been rude to listen in.

I had to get busy and get dressed for the day. I headed first to the All Mart to get my film developed. The same horrible intersection where town road ends and the state road towards the highway was as bad as ever. There was no other way to get to the All Mart. Hugh McMinn's truck wash was backed up with semis to the edge of the road. The measly stop sign at the end of the town road just wasn't enough. I had to scoot like a roadrunner from town road to the state road. At the All Mart I talked this nice young lady into only making me pay for the first two pictures to be developed. Those were the only ones on the disposable camera that I had taken. I had to kill an hour before the pictures would be ready. I figured by the time I returned home, Lilly would have hung up her end of the phone line.

When I got back from the All Mart, my phone was flashing with messages. First it was Lilly.

"Tiggy, Tiggy, TIGGY, are you there?" Then a bleep with no message, then Lib.

"Call me about what you are wearing tonight." Next it was Estelle.

"Tiggy, I just talked to Lilly, I wanna go tonight, B,Y." Next it was Hugh McMinn.

"Mrs. Adams, please call me if you ever have a problem, I am open to dialogue."

I thought to myself, you are full to the brim with phony baloney and a side of Blarney! I dialed the McMinns and hoped that pile of lalapalooza answered. Betty answered but she called him to the phone when I said I was returning a call from her husband.

Hugh got on the phone.

"Thank you for returning my call Mrs. Adams. How are you today?"

"Just fine." There was a long pause. I wasn't going to tap dance for him when he oughta beg for mercy.

"What I called you about was concerning your photographing us with our daughter earlier."

Pause effect still in my control.

He finally said, "Could you tell me what your objective was?"

"Certainly. My best friend and her dog were attacked by a black and brown dog last night. A dog they've never seen before. A dog that required both my friend and her prize winning Corgi to have stitches. This poses the need for the dog responsible to be quaran*tined*. Does that answer your question?"

"Well if you had talked to us we could have told you it wasn't Susan's dog."

"I did talk to you daughter and she seemed unwilling to volunteer the dog for identification."

He stammered. "If Susan's dog did anything it was without our knowledge."

"Whenever a dog is not on a leash and out of a confined and secure area, what they do **is** still the owner's responsibility. That is why we have LEASH laws. They force pet owners to protect people from the unpredictable behavior of dogs."

"I see we're not getting a resolution."

"You mean you are not hearing what you want. You and your family cannot run roughshod over little old ladies and their rights to safety. Your idea of resolution is for me to tell you it's O.K. for your daughter's dog to chew on us as doggie treats! Until people like you came into our town, it was a nice, safe, and friendly place. Now it's fraught with the likes of heartless, ill-bred people who only care about raising home prices and our property taxes!" He hung up.

I called Estelle and told her about the day's events. She asked me if I was bringing the photo of the McMinns dog to tonight's council meeting. I told her I was bringing that picture if I had to walk through fire to bring it. I told her I was in a dither to get dressed and feed Pookie. After I hung up I remembered I had told Lib to bring pictures of her hedge. I needed to look for pictures from Mattie's wake too. Funny, (not funny ha,ha) how Mattie's funeral coincided with the end of life as we once knew it in Mountain Empire. Her empty house started the whole onslaught of incomers.

I called Lib to remind her about the hedge pictures. Next I called Lilly.

"Tiggy, how are you dressing? Pants or a skirt?"

"Lilly, I'm dressing to kill!"

She laughed.

"Seriously, I'm wearing my Liz pantsuit, the navy one. And my black pearls."

"I think I'll wear my red suit. It gives me courage and energy."

"Do that Lilly, just don't forget the pictures." Then I called Estelle to tell her what Lilly and I were wearing tonight. She said she was going to wear her red shell, red and white seersucker slacks and red sandals. I hung up and charged into the living room to look through my box of photos. I reminisced as I looked at old garden club pictures of Mattie, Lilly, Estelle, Lib and Me. I stopped and froze for a moment. There was a picture of Mattie and her ex-husband. I stared at him thinking, I had seen him only yesterday. I told myself to stop thinking crazy.

I picked up Lib first, in case I needed extra help with getting Lilly in the car. Lilly was having a lot of trouble with stairs. She had the living room sofa made out like a bed. The first thing she said was, "I have only had a put-put bath. I can't get in the shower until day after tomorrow. I need to know if I put too much Red on."

I stopped for a moment because she was wearing red. We both laughed at ourselves, she was referring to her perfume, also called Red.

"You wear all the red you want!"

"I've got my pictures Tiggy."

Lilly and Lib both asked at the same time, "You have my pictures don't you Tiggy?"

"Don't worry, the pictures are in my purse."

"I wanna see that dog of the McMinn's." I handed the envelopes over to her. While she located the right picture, we headed to pick up Estelle.

I certainly was glad I hadn't sold the old LTD. It was roomy and solid as a tank. Lilly practically caused me to wreck the car.

"That's the one, that's him! Thank God, and I say it reverentially, you got him!" I told Lilly,

"You are gonna have to take this picture over to the police and fill out a complaint. At least make them pay what you owe Doc Wiley."

"But he didn't charge me a thing."

"Well," make him give you a bill Lilly! Then why don't you go over to Charlottesville and tell a psychologist you have "big dog" phobia now."

We all laughed and started singing the fight song from the local High School football team: Who Let The Dogs Out.

As we got uptown, I started to park in a handicap spot so Lilly could have an easier time getting in the building.

"Guys, I'm just going to let all of y'all out here in the front. I'll park around the corner."

Lib got out first and helped Lilly over the curb. Some stranger in a big SUV honked, then whizzed around me. I looked up long enough to see them glaring at me. I pulled around to park but the SUV had taken up one and a half spaces. I had to park down another whole block. I composed myself and adjusted my pearls back around so the clasp didn't show and marched on.

Lib, Estelle and Lilly were waiting for me at the elevator. Lib asked, "What'd you do, go home and park?"

"I had to park a few more blocks away than I'd planned, but I'm here and that's all that counts."

I wanted to save my energy for a battle worth fighting. We got to the meeting room and sat in the middle row. I quickly took an aisle seat on the other side. I whispered to Lilly, Lib and Estelle, "This way we can be seen and heard easier."

Lilly said, "But you are a better spokesman."

"Don't worry, just follow my lead."

There I sat on the aisle seat in my Liz suit and black pearls. Lilly was in the opposite aisle seat in bright red and absolutely reeking of Red. Estelle sat next to Lilly, in her red sleeveless shell, humongous white beads and matching earrings, clutching her summer white bag like she was a courier for Wells Fargo. Lib was in a bright yellow cotton pantsuit with little frogs embroidered all over the pants. She was layered in Windsong, a perfume she bought at a half price sale at the drugstore. I had no doubt she had bathed, powdered, and sprayed herself to the point of saturation. Anyone who didn't notice us that night had to of been deaf, dumb and blind.

Mayor Hunt was seated in the middle of the head table like always. Every member of council seemed engrossed in reading something. It was time to start, straight up seven. No sight of Mr. Nibruska of the Historical Committee. Just then, Hugh McMinn walked in and took the seat at the table where Nibruska had sat the month before. This time, Rev. Somebody from the Ever Lasting Faith church opened with prayer. It was the big guns for invoking the Almighty tonight. I guess council realized if we ever needed prayer, it was now. Then the minutes from the last meeting were read and I started feeling red. Every member of council looked out with an expression on their face as if they were waiting for a reprieve from death row. I leaned over and looked pointedly at Lilly. I sat charm school straight and they took my cue to do the same. Then Lamarr asked if there was any new business.

Jimmy Knorr stood up first, Mary Lou sat beside him. "Lamarr, as you know, Mama was here a month ago with a request for a variance from the council concerning her roof."

Everybody was holding their breath.

"Upon returning the night of last council meeting, as y'all all know, it was raining to beat the band. Mama came home to so many roof leaks we didn't have enough pots to catch them. I subsequently got on her roof to lay a boat tarp. This further broke other slates, thin and fractured from their age. It became imperative to act. At my insistence,(Mary Lou stood up next to her son), Mama let me, a licensed roofer, remove and replace her roof the next day. Two days later, the Historical Review Committee confirmed in a letter to Mama (Mary Lou raised the letter in her hand) that under ordinance 1455-B they were placing a lien on her house for the cost of a metal roof."

I had heard it was for a slate roof. Be that as it may, we all knew she couldn't afford a metal one either."

Jimmy continued, "According to state law, and I have a copy right here for all y'all, if a deed holder in a historic district purchased their home before Architectural covenants were included in the deed, said covenants cannot be enforced provided the covenants place a financial, mental or physical hardship on the deed holder. Mr. Mayor and council, I am hereby submitting a letter from Mama's doctor, and copies of her previous tax returns, proving this lien has caused her blood pressure to soar and her yearly income is below the cost of a metal roof. What you people, (he pointed at Hugh) have tried to do is illegal, not to mention…, well, it's just plain immoral."

The mayor and the council did their mime troupe thing again. Hugh McMinn started patting his foot to the floor like he had a nervous tick. Jimmy walked up and handed every council member a copy of the papers they brought.

Hugh McMinn said, "These covenants were publicized for a period of thirty days prior to being passed into city statutes." Before he could say another thing, I motioned for the fab four(Lilly, Estelle, Lib and me) to stand up. We stood up in all our perfumed glory.

"Mr. McMinn, these statutes are after the fact of this state law Jimmy just told you about. You and your Historical committee shouldn't have even written a law that didn't contain the same requirements as the state!"

Everybody that was a citizen of Mountain Empire, stood up and yelled, "Take the lien off Mary Lou, she's our friend and your friend too!"

That wasn't exactly the diddy Estelle had come up with but it was close enough. Lamarr began talking back and forth to the council. The chanting for Mary Lou continued, and our fab four clapped along. Then the microphone squealed, Lamarr leaned back in pain,"Quiet please! Please stop singing, we are out of order!"

Jimmy turned around and waved us to sit down. "Thank you folks, let's see if the mayor has a good word for us."

Lamarr cupped his hand over the mike and said something to Hugh. Then Lamarr said, "The lien is hereby removed and variance is granted for an asphalt shingle roof for 305 Central Avenue." Then the mayor said, "Jimmy, Tiggy, all y'all, would you please take down those signs?" We all laughed and nodded. Then he said, "Is there any more new business?" Before I could get back to my feet, Hugh McMinn spoke.

"The Historical Review Committee announces that the Ivy Heights subdivision is now under temporary statute as the Ivy Heights Historic District, subject to the same covenants as the Main Street Historic district."

Those were fightin words and I don't mean maybe. Before the time slipped by, I was going to get my two cents in about the dogs ruining Lib's hedge. I also intended to bring up the menace from loose dogs. Everybody from Ivy Heights pro and con for being the newest Historic designee was buzzing.

Brett Wytheville stood up,

"Mr. Mayor we have a petition from a quorum of residents in Ivy Heights. Our petition is to prevent our neighborhood from becoming another designated Historic District."

Then another resident of Ivy Heights stood up and said, "Ivy Heights is a unique community. It's not that the people don't want progress, but we want it with one thing staying the same. We want the option of being historic property to be decided on a house to house basis. These codes devised by Mr. McMinn and his comrades are too strict. If anything, many of our homes could fall into disrepair with the costly requirements of "period" elements."

Lamarr leaned into the mike.

"Ladies and gentlemen, due to time constraints, we will take up the matter of a qualifying statute regarding the status of Ivy Heights as a Historic District next month. Now we are going to address what to do about all the sink holes popping up all over downtown."

I didn't know whether to kiss him or kill him. Miss Mary Lou was saved from ruin but I wanted to show the pictures and Lilly's leg. Here we were, Estelle, Lib, Lilly and me, all dressed up and no one to dress down. It sure took the winds out of our sails. Lamarr hit the gavel, turned off his mike and turned to talk to someone beside him. Lilly looked at me and gave me a "what now?" look. I went over to the three of them. "Well, I've a good mind to block the door."

Estelle said, "Now Tiggy, don't have a hissy fit. We are given out tonight, not given up." Truer words were never spoken.

5 IDLE THREATS

The next day, the paper was full of what had happened with Miss Mary Lou's situation. It was Jimmy and Hugh McMinn the paper quoted the most. I don't blame Mary Lou for letting Jimmy do her "heavy lifting" in dealing with all that mess. Hugh McMinn was lucky as a rainbow Lilly and I didn't get to present our evidence about what his daughter's dog had done. You can bet your life if we had, Lilly and I would have been quoted up one side and down the other of today's paper. The Letters to the editor were overwhelmingly in favor of the decision to grant the variance to Mary Lou. Dr. Oscar Wiley also wrote a very powerful letter in the editorial section against Ivy Heights becoming another historic district. It read, "Eighty percent of our community are longtime residents. They have given me the go ahead to state clearly and categorically we are tired of what this Historical Committee has tried to dictate as to what people can and cannot do to their homes. Historical Review committee has approved radical changes for themselves and discriminated against those of us who have been citizens of Mountain Empire all our lives. Case in point; Mr. Nibruska, the chairman for the Historical Review Committee put an asphalt shingle roof on his house in our neighborhood, while denying the same roof to an elderly resident in West Beverley. I realize we are not designated as a historic district yet, however Mr. Nibruska would gain much respect by observing the same requirements he has tried to force on others."

I mused out loud, "Bravo Doc Wiley!" He went on to state he had heard of one lady in the East Beverley area who was prohibited from repainting her house in the existing blue, because her style of home could only be painted in earth tones. I knew he was referring to Estelle. Then he posed a very relevant argument for vinyl siding and vinyl replacement windows. He said, "If Abraham Lincoln and Robert E. Lee could have had vinyl siding and windows that didn't require painting, wouldn't they have preferred it?"

Another letter was from someone complaining about the new tax assessments that would be coming in January. He claimed to know they would be up thirty percent in some areas. I put the paper down and called city hall and asked the operator for the city assessor. It was busy for the next five times I tried. I became frustrated and finally left a message on the tax assessor's voice mail for him to call me back. Then I read another letter from someone who said, "I would like to blow these upstart, elitist yuppies of the Historical Review Committee back to the stone age!" It was signed: Will

B. Justice. It had to be a joke, I didn't know of anybody in the county named Justice. When the tax assessor returned my call, He told me I was one of many residents concerned about our new tax hikes. He confirmed the new rates would indeed be up thirty percent in our area. Ivy Heights would also have between a twenty and twenty five percent increase. The rest of the town would be up too. He said this was due to the meteoric rise in the contract sales price for homes in our designated historic district.

"Miz Adams, are you aware the six member Historical Review Committee is subject to election every two years? If you pay the one hundred fifty dollars per year to belong to the Mountain Empire Historical Society you and your friends can run for seats on the Review committee?"

"Why no, how…- - WHY, is this not more public?"

"Because you and most of the original residents have not bothered to investigate their charter. It would behoove you to come to my office for all the information regarding this committee."

"Mr. Creel, I will be down to your office in two shakes. Just make a copy of everything concerning the Historical Society and Review Committee, and leave it at the reception area please." "Mighty fine Miz Adams, and good luck to you and yours."

I thanked him and hit the ground running.

Pookie hadn't had more than a walk out the back door, she was dancing around thinking we were on our way.

"Sorry Pookie, I'm on a mission, no time to walk today!"

I dressed in a hurry and barely remembered to put on my lipstick. I was going to need a half inch off my hair. When I showered tonight, I would give myself a trim. I leashed Pookie and stood at the back door while she tinkled one more time in the yard and then headed out. As I drove out the alley and turned to go down my street, I noticed as I passed the "Pookay"/ Pucketts, an appliance truck from Pete Gwaltney's store was parked in their driveway. The very people who suggested one night a week every house built before electricity should operate on candle light and gas lanterns. What a bunch of hypocrites.

The one and only time I saw the inside of the house after the Pucketts bought it was when I took them a welcome dinner. The Pucketts were having walls erected in the upstairs hall in order to put two extra bathrooms. The new second floor bath room chopped up the hallway above the front entry. When the toilet flushed, you could hear it plain as day while standing inside the front door. The Pucketts were trying to make the house into something it wasn't. They were especially proud to have matching furniture ensembles in every room. It had the look of what can only be described as a Victorian funeral parlor. The mood was completed with dark upholstery and drapes, dark painted walls, stuffed birds in a glass case and the piece de resistance: A female mannequin dressed in full Victorian regalia posed in the front window downstairs. Next to the mannequin was a huge Victorian bird cage centered in the front window with a live Macau as its resident. The only daylight I saw came from where the bird cage and mannequin stood. You'd have thought they slept all day, only came out at night and had an aversion to crosses. They gave me the creeps. And to think they tried to make folks believe their name was pronounced "Pookay"! If they want to be called "Pookay", then I could honestly call them the "spookay Pookays". At least Pete's store was getting their business, for he was struggling to compete with the Home Improvement Warehouse by the highway.

As I reached uptown, I was able to park a few spaces from the entrance to city hall. "Alright, that's more like it." I said to myself. Mr. Creel had left a brown envelope with my name on it, at the reception desk. I thanked the receptionist and headed back to my car. I remembered I was nearly out of gas, so I stopped at Mr. Krishna's station. I waved at him as he sat inside the old rounded bay window. He returned the gesture but just went on with whatever he was doing. It never occurred to me he wouldn't come out and pump my gas. I waved him out from inside my car.

"Yes Meese?"

"Hello there Mr. Krishna, are you not pumping gas at all any more?" He pointed to the big self-serve sign and said no, it was all self-serve.

"Then there is nowhere in town for a lady to get her car serviced!"

"I am cheaper because I no serve."

"Figure what it would cost me to have you put my gas in." He looked up at the overhang for a minute.

"It would be three more dollars."

"Three more dollars it is, let her rip!" He looked at me strangely but obliged my request. It was worth the three dollars not to get dirty and smelly from gasoline. After he finished I gave him the money and he leaned in my driver's window.

"Meese, my name eez Deepend-rah, Kreeshna Deepend-rah."

Then he smiled and bowed as he stepped back on the gas pump island. I liked him after that.

I had no more gotten in the back door when my phone rang. The message light showed several messages. It was Estelle. "Thank heavens your home. Lilly and I both have been trying to reach you."

"What's happened now?

"Well, first off, Lilly is down in the dumps and I don't mean maybe. Doc Wiley saw her today and immediately referred her to the hospital."

"What's wrong!?"

"That place on her leg is going to have a scar unless the plastic surgeon can do something. Worse yet, Beaucoup is going to have a visible scar too."

"Oh no Estelle, what about the dog show at the Salem Civic Center?"

"That's the thing Tiggy, Lilly doesn't care about her leg, it's Beaucoup's blue ribbons he won't ever have again that's bothering her."

That just beat all. First it was the trouble and expense of getting injured and now insult to injury.

"I was telling Pete about it. He said Hugh was liable because the dog was staying at his property."

"But Estelle, Lilly has to sign a complaint. Has she done that yet?"

"Well, she was hoping you would take her to do that."

I told her I would call Lilly right now. We hung up and I started to dial but decided to see what my messages were. The first two were hang ups, the next was Lilly, the next was a hang up and the next was Estelle. The last one was a voice I didn't recognize. It sounded male but I wasn't a hundred percent sure. 'It' said, "Darla and Bill Puckett are 'doing it' at the vacant house on Central Ave."

I didn't have caller I.D. or I would have known the number they were calling from. I called the phone company and they told me my service included something called star sixty nine. After they explained what to do, I dialed it. It rang and rang and rang. Finally, someone answered it.

"Highway Hamburgers." I was taken aback.

"Uh, yes this is Mrs. Archie Tigley Adams, did you call me?" They told me it was the payphone in the hall by the restrooms. "Well, someone called me, could you ask around, I'll wait." "Ma'am, I just came on shift. You can't see the phone from the registers. We have people come off the highway exit to eat and use this payphone all day and night."

"Oh, I see, well, thank you anyway."

Then I remembered, Judy McMinn had a house listed on Central but it was preposterous to think Bill Puckett would be trysting with someone there. Of course, just maybe, if it was going on after midnight, it was because he needed some more blood. He was a painter though, not a realtor. I thought it was probably a prank. My curiosity was up so I decided to pay Miss Mary Lou a visit. I would nonchalantly ask her who had been in the vacant house. I called Miss Mary Lou and stood there for near eternity, waiting for her to answer. When she finally answered I told her I wanted to bring something to her and visit. She was very receptive, since everybody knows I am one of the best cooks in this town. I set the time for a half hour later.

Then I called Martha Lofton realty and asked for Shelby Ann. They transferred me to her cell phone which had the most obnoxious message.

"This is Shelby Ann, your home maker, dream maker." Then she sang: "leave your name and number and the time you called too, as soon as I am free, I'll be calling you."

I hung up quick as a wink. That display of the ego that ate Atlanta was just too much for me. I called Lofton realty back and asked the receptionist what she could tell me about the listing on Central. After she gave me price and blah, blah, blah, I asked her what realtors could let me in to see it. She said, Martha Lofton, Bill Puckett or Betty McMinn, or the HomeMaker :Shelby Wytheville.

"You say Bill Puckett? Is he a realtor too?

She said he was only part time but a full time realtor would be glad to show me the house or any other. I begged off pretending I would think about it. Now my curiosity was up. Who and why would someone call me and say such a tacky thing about Darla and Bill Puckett?

I opened my freezer, looking for a nice casserole. I found a Chicken Tetrazini and placed it in one of the paper grocery bags I had saved. I carried the bag to the car and headed to Mary Lou Knorr's. She was glad to see me, and took the bag from me like it was a trophy. I followed her into the kitchen as she took the casserole out of the bag and put it on the counter to thaw. She started to throw the bag away.

"Oh, Miss Mary Lou, if you don't mind I'd like to keep the bag. I have to drive towards the interstate to All Mart in order to get one that size. I always cook my turkey in a paper bag, coated with olive oil. Have you ever tried that?"

She gave me the look of astonishment. I get that from everybody unfamiliar with the superior flavor it gives.

Everything in her kitchen had a cozy on it. The vacuum cleaner had a cozy made to look like a French maid but with the face of the late Julia Childs. The toaster had a cozy resembling a pig, complete with curly tail. The hand mixer and bowl had one that looked like an iced cake with a cherry on top. I then remembered, every bottle on the sink counter in her guest bath had hand crochet doll cozies with neon red hair. I was too afraid to ask her where they all came from for fear she had made them. No one in their right mind would pay good money for anything as atrocious as that. She offered me some caffeine free tea. She looked around for the tea kettle and tea pot. At her age, I would have at least taken the cozy off the water kettle just for safety's sake. I don't know how she ever found a darned thing. The water kettle was covered in a cozy made to look like a curled up cat. After playing hide and seek with the cozies covering the kettle, sugar bowl and container of sweet and low, we finally had a cup of cat, frog, apple and bell pepper tea. For it was under that many cozies, she scavenged for the makings of two cups of tea! It was exhausting just to watch her. As we settled into her living room I could see the house for sale three doors down. Mary Lou began our conversation by thanking me for the support I lent at the council meeting. I assured her it was my pleasure. I asked her if she had read today's paper and the letters to the editor. She wanted to talk about what Doc Wiley had said. Then she mentioned the one from Mr. "Justice".

I asked casually, "Have there been many lookers at the house down the street?"

"Oh there have been a slew of them."

"I understand Bill Puckett is a part time realtor now too." "He is over there usually in the evening with customers. One lady has been there two nights this week. I can't see too well at night, but the lady looking at the house brings this big, black dog with her. Several times this summer, my grandson has complained about the dog mess left from on my front yard. He cuts my grass you know."

I tried to compose my expression.

"How many times has this one lady looked at the house? Me, I know if I like a house on the first look."

She stopped and thought as if this was the first time she had wondered about it.

"You know Tiggy, the lady with the dog has come at least three times this month.

Maybe she has already put in an offer, do you spose?"

"Oh yes, that must be it." I said with great restraint.

Then she said something that interested me in a different way.

"I heard that the Nibruska's house was insured very little over what they paid and now with the fire and all they have lost a pretty penny."

"Well Miss Mary Lou, if you come in to town and pay one price, then do all those remodelings, you oughta have sense enough to raise your insurance."

I asked her if she had heard anything about who loaned them the fans that caused the fire. She didn't know anything more than I did, which was a whole lot of nothing.

"Well, thank you for the tea. I hope you put that casserole to good use."

Actually, I was going to need the use of a bathroom after all that tea. I wanted to get back home where finding the toilet paper wouldn't turn into a scavenger hunt.

I came away knowing more than I wanted to this time. It disturbed me that Darla might have gotten herself mixed up with the likes of a man as strange as Bill Puckett. His wife had cussed out every person who did work on their house more than once. Carter told me she was a shrew and a half, and used awful language as a matter of habit. Darla had bitten off more than she could chew again if it was true. I for one, wouldn't have been on a first name basis with Bobby, much less share a bed. We were due to have our annual Labor Day neighborhood party in a month or so. It was a toss of a coin now just how neighborly it would turn out to be.

I got in the back door after visiting Mary Lou to find Pookie dancing around. Either she was glad to see me or in need of relief too. I ran in the guest bath under the stairs and yelled.

"Don't worry precious, I'm taking you for a walk."

I threw on my walking shoes and headed out. It was down the alley and around the corner. Then, up East Beverley in the direction of Lib's. As I got to Lib's house, I spied her wearing her late husband's old shirt and some Bermuda shorts. She had a geeky looking young man with her and he was pruning her hedge. She turned and spoke to me and told me she wanted me to meet someone.

"Tiggy, this is Jay Bradford, a horticulturist from Virginia Tech's Agriculture Dept. He's a graduate assistant and he even knows how to make a bonsai tree!"

The young man was extremely shy and awkward. When I asked him what he thought could be done about the boxwoods, he began to pontificate. After getting a dissertation which I understood half of, I turned to Lib somewhat impatiently.

"Have you registered a complaint of vandalism with the police yet? You better do it before you let him cut the evidence away." She told the young man to give her fifteen minutes before resuming pruning. Then she told me she was going straight to the police and register a complaint in order to have animal control on her side. I told her as soon as I gave Pookie a walk, I was taking Lilly down to make her report too.

When Pookie and I made our way home, I called Lilly.

"O.K., I'm dressed and I'll take you to talk to the police anytime between now and then."

"Give me five minutes. Just pull up in back and honk."

I put my sandals back on and headed to Lilly's. Lilly came out wearing an old Laura Ashley sun dress. It was just below the knee, and her legs were stained like dried blood. It looked like she'd cut them shaving. I looked at the front of her legs in horror.

"I know what you're thinking Tiggy, but it's sunless tanning lotion. I was trying to make these fish belly, white legs, look less scary."

I wasn't going to say a word that wasn't true, but she had not applied the stuff right. It looked like she had poured orangey-brown paint, willy nilly, down her legs and feet.

We headed to town and I asked her how she was feeling. She seemed down in the dumps after I asked.

"Lilly, we don't have to talk about this incident if you don't want to."

"It's O.K. Tiggy, but Beaucoup's winning streak is over. I'm going to take his blue ribbons and have them framed professionally. His leg is visibly scarred from that awful dog of Susan McMinns. I can't enter him in any more competitions looking like that."

I knew from Estelle she was going to have a scar if she wasn't careful. I made no mention of it, she just needed to talk.

At the police station, the lady at the front desk listened to Lilly as she asked for an officer. The woman was dressed in a uniform like a policeman but she did nothing but answer the phone. She asked Lilly in a nasal voice to explain what she needed to see an officer about. She seemed completely detached as she listened to Lilly. I half way wished I could find out who the woman was. I doubt she was from any family I was acquainted with. She treated us as if we were strangers. Anyhow, she called for the floor officer and he came out. I told Lilly to show him her leg and remind him an officer had come out a few days before and wrote something down. Just then, Lib came out from down the hall. She came up to us and remarked how bad Lilly's legs looked. I whispered it was only one leg injured but that she had put sunless tan lotion on like incomers painted rooms. Her legs looked like they had a "faux" finish.

The officer excused himself and went back behind a door. A few minutes later he came out with a report and asked Lilly to verify it. Lib begged off for home and I sat listening. Lilly then gave him the photo of the dog and a photo of her leg and Beaucoup's.

"You see officer, my dog receives two hundred dollars a night for stud fees because he is a Best in Show champion. Now he will never be able to perform in competitions again."

The officer winced when he found out who's dog had done the dirty deed. I could tell he knew something about how arrogant Hugh was.

"Mrs. Wiley, I will get a warrant for the dog to appear for official identification. You will have to sign an affidavit as to the surety of your identification of the subject dog. Then your neighbor's daughter, or whoever owns the dog, will have to relinquish the animal for ten days quarantine. Are you willing to see it through to a court date if I get the ball rolling?" "I certainly will sir!"

Then he stood up and wished us a good day and thanked us for coming in. The rude woman at the desk never looked up. We left feeling relief.

Lilly said, "I hope the McMinns have to pay for the ten days quarantine and not our tax dollars."

As we left the police parking lot, Estelle and Pete rode by with both little girls in the back. We waved at each other. I asked Lilly if she had heard anything lately about Darla. She said no, but that Estelle told her Pete was still bitter about the divorce. Then Lilly said she was glad Darla was on the straight and narrow after the ruckus she had already caused by marrying Bobby. I remembered the feelings of Pete and Darla's little girls. I wasn't about to mention my crank caller so I told Lilly she must be right.

That evening I had a lean cuisine for supper and settled in to watch a little television. Halfway through a Hallmark movie, the phone rang. I thought about not answering since I rarely had a moment's peace as of late. I answered and it was the "it" voice.

"They're doing it again at 300 Central." Then they hung up. I quickly dialed the star sixty nine. It told me what my last incoming call was. I dialed the number quick as I could. It rang and rang, no answer. I hung up and the phone rang again. This time I wasn't going to be nice about it. I picked up the phone.

"Now look *here*." and Estelle said, "Tiggy, Tiggy?"

"Oh, Estelle, I thought you were a crank caller."

"Well, obviously something's wrong!" I told her it was nothing, just some kid. I sure wasn't going to tell her what the crank caller said either.

She told me she was going to the city hall the next day to get a list of colors approved for the outside of her house. She didn't want any trouble from Historic Review committee. I halfway listened and made an excuse to get off the phone. "Estelle, how about I call you tomorrow and we'll put our heads together before you talk to Nibruska?"

"There's no getting around those approved colors, no exception or anything like that. Pete's already called the state people."

"Estelle, I just want to make sure we make a statement about our misgivings on the intrusiveness of all these doggone rules!" "Tiggy, I'll just let your brain do its thing, if anybody can make the Historical Committee cry uncle it's you."

"I thank you for your vote of confidence. Now call me first thing tomorrow. O.K Estelle?" We hung up and I grabbed Pookie's leash.

She bounded from her bed by the fridge.

"Well girl, don't bark til you see the whites of their eyes."

I headed out the front door, towards Central Ave like I was on my way to a fire. There was no one out and daylight was quickly waning into darkness. I wish daylight savings time was in effect all year. I enjoyed the red sky on my walk even though it meant a hot day tomorrow. One more block to go and we would cross to Central. People were sitting out on their front porches. All the incomers had lit scented candles on their porches. There were a half dozen aromas wafting through the air between the candles, Gardenia bushes and fabric softener from someone's dryer. I headed down the sidewalk next to the Pookay/Pucketts. The house was dark as usual except for a small spot light on the eerie mannequin. There was no sign of the Macau in the cage.

I passed Mary Lou's house and could see the television flashing intermittently from the side window in back. Right when we got to 300 Central Ave, I slowed down to let Pookie sniff. I didn't want to blow my cover. I looked for signs of life inside 300 Central but there were no lights on. As I was concentrating on the house, I stepped in a pile of horse size droppings left on the sidewalk. I quickly got on the grass to wipe my feet and Pookie walked around me almost tripping us both.

"Sugar! Pookie, stay, STAY!" I whispered angrily. I finally got untangled and heard a dog bark from inside the dark, vacant house. Pookie's bark tape went off and all you could hear was competition between her yip, yip and the other dog's low, throaty bark. Just then, Pete Gwaltney came from the end of the block with Jenny and

Beaucoup. I grabbed Pookie up and held her mouth to keep her quiet and composed myself.

"Oh Pete, how nice of you to help Lilly out."

He smiled and said, "Mrs. Wiley is afraid to walk after dark for fear of falling and hurting her stitches." He kept up his pace and went by quickly.

"Enjoy your evening." He hurriedly said out of the side of his mouth. He was really bookin' it. I felt like a certified idiot standing there holding Pookie's mouth to keep her quiet.

I was still trying to wipe the crud off my yard sandals when Bobby Tatum drove by the opposite way. He turned around in a driveway and pulled up at 300 Central. He parked there with his engine running and gunned the motor with the broken muffler that would wake the dead. I could just see the headlines in tomorrow's paper: Love triangle, no, make that: Love rectangle(for this had even more sides) ends in bloody shoot out in Historic District.

I turned around and power walked back the way I came. I stopped to look back and heard someone pounding on the front door of 300. I guess it was Bobby, his truck was still running. I was still holding Pookie as I sprinted home, wondering if I should call the police and report a murder to be. I fumbled with my key and burst into the front door. Quickly I locked up and put windows down on my first floor. This time I put all my outside lights on front and back. Then I went upstairs so I could watch out my bathroom window to the alley. After a few minutes, I went ahead and put on my nightgown. It wasn't until around eleven forty five P.M. that I heard Bobby's truck. Tired as I was, I just had to see if Darla was with him. She was at her back door in a bathrobe as she and Bobby exchanged angry words. She wouldn't let him past the screen door, that much was obvious. I didn't understand all I knew about the situation. Who was the "it" person who called. Someone wanted to make trouble for Darla. Darla seemed more than able to make trouble for herself and that's for darn sure.

6 ARCHITECTURALLY CORRECT

The next morning, I overslept after tossing and turning. I had barely gotten out of bed before the phone rang. I hurried to the downstairs where my only portable phone was. It was Estelle, the last person I wanted to talk to. I was trying to get the leash on Pookie before she took her break in routine out on my floor.

"Good morning, you sound half asleep."

"I am, I overslept by a mile. Now I'm getting Pookie out to water the grass before she waters the kitchen floor." I talked as I headed out the back door, still holding on to Pookie's leash.

"Well Tiggy what did your overactive imagination come up with last night?"

I winced, knowing some of the things from last night were anything but my imagination. I brought Pookie back in and still couldn't collect myself.

"Estelle, let me have one cup of coffee so my head won't be clear as mud. I promise to call you right back, promise!"

"O.K., B,Y!"

For once in her life she gave me a pass without asking questions.

I started the coffee and sat down to clear my head. Did I get that crazy call last night? Yes, but was it really anything to worry about? Should I be the one to spill the beans, if there really is something going on between Darla and Bill Puckett? Estelle had been through enough as had her granddaughters. I should just sit on this for a while; it could all be innocent. On the other hand, where there's smoke there is usually fire. There must be something going on between Darla and Bill or Darla and Bobby. I wondered if Estelle was as in the dark as her demeanor on the phone indicated.

I couldn't stand to think about it anymore until I'd had my coffee. As I sipped it, I smelled something, something awful. I looked around for the source. There by the back door were my yard sandals, still crusted from that foul and inconsiderate dog owner. Then I was jolted back to the reality that I had acted foolishly. Tearing out of the house like that, just because of a crank call. I thought about why Estelle might have phoned me, I'd bet money it was about painting her house. I dialed her number and she answered bright and cheerfully.

"Estelle, when are you going down to city hall to pick up your approved house colors?"

"Well, I'm glad you remembered. I was thinking maybe you would want to go with me. That way we can both get our list." Oh joy of joys I thought.

I told her I needed a shower and a short walk with Pookie. It was already eight-fifteen. She asked me if I could be ready by nine, when the offices would be open uptown. I told her fine and then hung up. I put on my yard clothes and fastened Pookie's leash on and we headed out the back door as usual. As I came through my gate, there was Bobby Tatum throwing equipment helter skelter into one of his trucks. He acted like he didn't see me and I assumed the same posture. I looked around warily for his dog, it was sitting in the front seat of the truck. It was a pleasure nowadays to have the freedom to walk down our alley with Gus restrained. I started to hum something from the latest television ad that had struck a chord in my brain. I looked back at Bobby as we headed out of the alley. He looked up at me momentarily, red as a beet in the face, even his ears.

I decided to retrace my route from the previous evening. As I got to Lib's, she was out putting SNAIL AWAY around her boxwoods. I said good morning to her and she half hollered back: "Let's get all the girls together and rent a movie this weekend." "I walked and conversed at the same time.

"Sounds good- call me."

I got to the walkway on the side of the Pookay/Pucketts and noticed she was loading her big SUV with luggage. I just couldn't resist asking, "Going on vacation?"

She gave me her usual sour look and didn't even answer. That spoke volumes to me. The son looked down at the ground and didn't look up. I could see the Macau perched in his cage. The mannequin still had the spotlight on her, which was usually off in the morning.

Now I was beginning to think the 'it' who called was telling the truth, distasteful as it was. Pookie and I took a shortcut home in order to be ready on time. I dressed for comfort in my new white Liz jeans and a sleeveless shell with a deep V in the back and a small one in front. I put on my pearls and small silver loops, then blew my hair dry with a little mousse. I called Estelle from the upstairs phone to see if she expected me to drive but there was no answer. Pookie barked at the back door and I knew it must be Estelle. Before I could get downstairs, I heard her. She had let herself in with a key I had given her. She hollered, "I'm a little early, you ready?"

I came down and half expected her to ask me about what Bobby was doing. I asked her if she had any trouble getting around all of Bobby's trucks and junk. She said there was no one in the alley. I dropped the subject like a hot potato, as if nothing was going on.

I had no proof of anything, just a whole lot of speculation on my part so far.

"Now tell me what your brain has come up with today."

"Oh, I just want to see what color a Prairie style home and a Colonial Revival can be painted to start with."

"Is that all Tiggy, you shore you don't have some kind of plan hatching in that crazy head of yours?"

I laughed, "Estelle, there is always an idea waitin to spring forth. I can't help it, it's my nature."

"Oh… Tiggy, have you heard Mr. Krishna is getting married?" I said no and looked quizzically.

"Is it a local girl?"

"Naw, it's an arranged marriage through his home town back in the land of blue turbans or wherever he's from."

I had forgotten when he first took over the gas station, he wore a blue rag wrapped around his head. He stopped wearing it when he bought the adjacent building. I said an arranged marriage wasn't that bad of an idea. Estelle agreed with me too. As we headed out the back door she said,

"If I could have arranged Pete's marriage it would have been to a girl from a more modest family. But it was only after Darla's father died and her mother remarried that her subsidies ended."

"Don't we know how that goes, Stelle; you can't depend on family money when a second wife comes in the picture."

She nodded and told me if Pete could just move on from the divorce, he would meet someone.

"Why don't you try to find the next Mrs. Pete Gwaltney?" She grinned from ear to ear at that one.

I asked her as we headed downtown how she knew about Mr. Dipendrah. She told me there was an engagement picture in the morning's paper. I hadn't even gone to the front porch to get mine that morning. Pookie and I had come back home through the back because I was curious to see if Bobby had moved his ladders. Fortunately they were gone but I still wasn't sure if it was permanent.

"Earth to Tiggy, come in Houston."

"Oh, yes, uh, what did Mr. Dipendrah's intended look like? What's her name and can you spell it?"

"She is more attractive than he, and her name is Ajinder something something."

"Well, we'll just have to get them something something for an engagement present. I'll bet then he'll pump our gas for free."

We both giggled and craned our necks down First Street looking for a good parking spot.

As we entered city hall, I saw where Historic Review Committee was now listed in the glass directory.

"Would you look at that Estelle. I'm halfway tempted to switch the room number with the office of solid wastes!"

I pointed with my purse and she read the room number out loud. We decided to take the stairs. There was no one in the office and the secretary in the office next to it told us their hours were not set. We asked where we could get what we needed and she sent us to the city planning department. They gave us the handout with a color chart for every kind of architecture. We both started reading the la-di-da heading: Architecturally appropriate exterior colors are vital to the authenticity of your home.

"Ye Gods and little catfishes, I know who I am and what period my house is without this bunch of put on."

We decided to take the elevator down.

"Estelle, this Historical Committee boils down to one thing and one thing only. These incomers are trying to manufacture their heritage from our old homes. As soon as one of them moves into an old house they act like they own the history of it. If you ask me they are assuming a heritage they were never born into. They're just a bunch of snob wannabees. I say, we are the original snobs and the others are made in China! We are not out to impress anybody but ourselves."

Estelle shook with silent laughter. As the elevator stopped, the people in the elevator with us stepped back and let us out first. They had a look of respect and wariness all at one time.

I suggested we go over to the Lick Skillet and have a cup of coffee and a homemade sweet roll. Estelle said if she did that she would use up her weight watcher's points for lunch. I reminded her of the entertainment value only Hazel could provide. "If we go there, no telling what Hazel can tell us."

Estelle got a gleam in her eyes, "I'm there!"

In a few minutes we were seated at a back booth. That's the beauty of a small town, everything is a five minute drive. The only exception being Chapman's grocery going out of business and grocery shopping was now out by the highway exit.

Hazel's niece waited on us and I told her to tell Hazel to be sure and join us for a minute. Hazel brought our sweet rolls over.

"How's everything in the wide world of sports today?"

We both said fine, and I asked her, "Have you heard anything interesting lately?"

She got a strained look on her face and I knew instantly what that was all about. With Estelle sitting there it was best to change the subject. I decided to share the news about Mr. Dipendrah.

"Have you heard about Mr. Dipendrah? He's getting married in…, when is it Estelle?"

"The paper said he was to be married right before Labor Day, in his hometown and don't ask me to pronounce it."

Hazel remarked that was nice.

She offered quickly as if to keep the subject changing. "The couple who bought Matties's old house seemed nice. He asked me all about Mattie and her first husband. You know, what kind of people they were. His wife said the house came with the furnishings. I guess there was no one to leave anything to, Mattie never having children and all. He told me he was going to leave things the same when I first met him."

"What did he ask about Mattie and John?"

"Well, he wanted to know if people had liked both Mattie and John. I told him yes. I told him the only reason John left Mountain Empire with his second wife was because Mattie probably wouldn't have given him a moment's peace. He asked if people thought badly of her husband leaving her like he did. I told him I had never heard an unkind thing about John except from Mattie. It's not that I didn't like Mattie, but you know how she did take to her sick bed over every little thing. Then he told me they were unsure which of the furnishings were from Mattie's side. That's where I drew a blank. Tiggy, I bet you'd know."

"The bedroom set was bought new after John and Halcey Ann left for Tampa. I heard Mattie sent the old one to John, C.O.D. Now, I happen to know their original bedroom suit was from old Miz Fisher too. Don't you remember? It was the latest look in 1930, and John claimed to have been born in that bed."

Estelle said, "Well you can see why Mattie didn't care to keep it."

Hazel said, "MM-hmmm."

"The dining room set came from old Miz Fisher's home place, the kitchen table was built in around 1952 when Mrs. Fisher Sr. remodeled the kitchen as a wedding present to John and Mattie. Don't forget, she lived with them until she passed in '62. That about covers it because I don't remember what Mattie's living room looked like. Remember? She had that adjustable hospital bed in the living room towards the end. The last ten years of Mattie's life, she claimed to have that disease where you have to sleep inclined so your breathing didn't stop. Surely, the new couple got rid of that monstrosity of a bed."

"Well if you get a chance, stop by their place and share what you know. They said they both came to Mountain Empire because they heard it was a friendly, old fashioned town."

"With pleasure! No other incomers came here to preserve what we were, only what we live in! It's nice to have a young couple with the right values."

After we had our mid-morning pick me up at the Lick Skillet, Estelle took me home. I told her I'd invite her in but I needed to look at all the material on the Historical Review Committee that Mr. Creel had given me.

"After I read through the section on painting the outside of your house, I'll call you, O.K.?

She said fine and dropped me off at the front door. I picked up my paper, wondering if all was quiet out back in the alley. I ran upstairs to the bathroom so I could see out the back window. Both of Bobby's ratty old trucks were still gone as well as the ladders and saw horses. I knew the neighbors would be glad of that. If I didn't see hide nor hair of him and his black beast in the next few days, we would have a nice Labor Day block party.

I took the envelope of information from Mr. Creel and opened it, briefly scanning for the pages I wanted to look at. The words Local Investment Tax Credit caught my eye. Stated in the covenants of Historical Review committee was a promise of a five year tax credit. Tax credits would be awarded to any home in a historic district-provided the improvements made were equal to or more than the assessed value of the property. Further, all improvements must be in keeping with the period of the architecture. It was obvious to me, even at the high prices many of the newest incomers paid, their assessed values were still very low. Now things made sense, as to why they were willing to spend so much money remodeling to a fare thee well. They automatically received a tax credit! No longtime citizen could receive that unless we remodeled and updated most of our homes. No wonder they were making bathrooms out of hallways and building elaborate porches that were never there in the first place.

I started to boil inside; I tell you I could have chewed nails right there on the spot! How dare Woody and Lamarr allow a five year reprieve on property taxes for these incomers! It was patently unfair to make it a five year give away. One year O.K., but five fudging years? Just like my mama used to say, "New Money is worthless without class." Those of us on retirement incomes were not prepared for the increase in property taxes headed our way as a Happy New Year present. We didn't have the ready cash from the sale of property in the big Yankee cities. That meant we couldn't make all the improvements they were making but we would have the higher taxes to pay. I certainly didn't want to spend money to make my kitchen look like 1927 when my house was built. To take up all the old linoleum and put back the porcelain sink and tile counters would have been nice. That would cost more than I could or would pay at this stage in life.

I wanted a drink and I'm not a drinker. I hadn't even had lunch for pity sake. It was rare for me to imbibe except at the annual Labor Day block party. I thought my eyes were gonna bug out of my head if I didn't calm down. I went into the dining room , opened the hutch and pulled out the Lochanora. My daughter brought it to me as a gift from her vacation in Scotland. It was a liqueur that could warm the bones and cool the temper. Lochanora was not sold in the United States so I saved it only for very special occasions. This time it was specifically to keep me from doing something I could go to jail for. I figured that fell under special occasion, for I rarely wanted to kill someone.

I flipped to the pages on approved exterior colors for my Colonial Revival. I could paint my house the very blue Estelle was prohibited from using. Estelle was confined to a dark green, light yellow, a reddish brown and what I thought was Baby Has the Stomach Virus brown. I poured another glass of Lochanora and gulped it down in a most unlady like fashion. It was close to noon and I was feeling a buzz. I kept reading and drinking, hoping there was some loophole. Neutrals such as white, gray, or beige were allowed on all types of architecture. The approved colors were to be used within one year when the Historical Review Committee deemed your property in disrepair. I didn't think Estelle had gotten a nasty gram about her peeling paint so I called her up. I poured another Lochanora as I waited for her to answer. This time I would sip it, Lord knows when I would need it again. Pete answered and I asked for his mother. She came to the phone and sounded a little strained.

"Do you want me to call you back when Pete's not around? 'Cause dear you better hold on to your hat when I tell you what I've found out!"

"Tiggy, I'll be over in half an hour, O.K?" I said fine and hung up.

I grabbed a table napkin to mark my place in the historical stuff. Then I picked up my local paper. I turned to the lifestyle page to get a look at Mr. Dipendrah's fiancé. I think he wrote the blurb underneath the picture. It read like my daughter's old first grade reader from 1961. I decided to get out the mixed nuts and put something in my stomach before I finished my glass of Lochanora. I turned to the editorials and list of local events. There was a picture of Hugh McMinn, Bill Nibruska and Mrs. Spookay Pookay. They were touting an open house and garden tour of the Beverley Historic District for the coming Christmas Season.

Sherwood Ave was the tour of choice before they started to get their paws on our property. I would inform Mrs. Pookay/Puckett when she got back from "vacation", original citizens of Beverley area have always decorated elaborately. I would like to tell her we got along fine before they came. Our Christmas lights were popular with the whole county. Mrs. Spookay Pookay was quoted:

"We are currently drawing up new guidelines for period correct holiday ornamentation for our homes in the district. We are asking for input on whether or not to allow fake greenery with live. Electric candle lights are easier and safer than real candles. Light displays should be limited to this type. Very few homes in this district were built at a time when electric lights were used."

So now she wanted to steal Christmas from us! I told Pookie, "If Lib wants to drape her boxwoods with lights and I want to put out my Frosty the Snowman family and they try to stop us, they're gonna have hell to pay! Estelle walked in the kitchen door next to me and Pookie wagged Hello. I swigged down the Lochanora.

"Talkin to Pookie and drinkin in the middle of the day! Where is Tiggy and what have you done with her?"

I handed her the paper. "Did you read this?"

She took it and the Lochanora from me. She marched to the dining room sideboard with my liquer, looking back at me like I had two heads. As she read the article about the Puckett who stole Christmas, it began to register on her face. Her mouth dropped open and her eyes got big as saucers.

"They can't do this can they?"

"We better get down to city hall and talk to Mr. Creel and find out how we can sss-stop em!" I swayed a little on my feet "Tiggy you couldn' go to the mail box like that. Keep eatin the mixed nuts and I'll make some coffee."

"Estelle, you haven't read the paint nonsense yet. By the way, have the Historical people written you a complaint about your paint peeling?"

"No, why?"

"Well, that's a relief. Once they do, you have a year to paint or you can be fined!"

In the haze of Lochanora, I envisioned the perfect way to get around the paint decree. We could paint our homes one of the neutrals, then paint polka dots in the approved colors across the front. They couldn't do a darn thing to stop us. I said out loud to the air, "Put that in your spookay Pookay and smoke it!"

"Oh no, the wheels are turning under the influence. Tiggy you are TWI, thinking while intoxicated."

I about fell off the chair as I got up and took a ceremonial bow.

"Estelle, never fear, Tiggy is here." Then I waved the literature in the air and said, Let me tell you how we're gonna beat those incomers at their own game."

I felt a little woozy. Estelle tried to hand me a cup of coffee. I waved the coffee away.

"First I need a little nappy."

Estelle helped me to the living room sofa and closed the curtains. I woke up at three thirty that afternoon to the phone ringing like Quasimoto's church bells. My teeth felt like they had sweaters on them.

It was Lilly.

"Tiggy, Estelle told me about the idea with the paints. There's just one problem honey. If we paint dots on the front of our houses, we'll have to pay the painter again to repaint after the dots have done their work. We gotta find out what it will cost before we go off hell bent for leather."

"Lilly, Jimmy Knorr and his sons will help us for nothing. I just know it!"

"Oh! You've got a point there. Why don't we have a small dinner and invite everybody who would stand with us?"

I was gulping down water while she was talking.

"Tiggy are you there?"

"I'm sorry Lilly, I was just getting a drink of water, I'm <u>so</u> thirsty!"

"I heard you might be………… are you alright now? Was there something else bothering you Tiggy?"

"Yes, but I'm fine now."

"Tiggy are you sure there isn't something else? Like the story going around town about Darla and Bill Puckett?"

"You heard that too?"

I didn't want to add my two cents for once. Then she told me Lib had heard about it from Shelby. It seems the 'it' caller must have also called Mrs. Puckett. Mrs.

Puckett went to Lofton Realty and demanded to know who her husband had shown the house on Central to. According to Lilly, who heard it from Lib, Mrs. Spookay Pookay told them she was not going to have her husband showing houses in the evening. It took him away from their dinner hour. When the receptionist told her she had no control over showings, Mrs. Puckett treated the lady like dirt. She insisted on seeing the showing ledger. Then asked the receptionist what Darla Tatum looked like. That got everybody's attention in the office of course. Mrs. Puckett asked if anybody knew if her husband had ever shown it to Darla at any time. Shelby told Lib it put everybody in an awkward position. Getting no information from the receptionist, supposedly Mrs. Puckett just stormed out.

"Lilly I've heard Mrs. Puckett has a terrible temper."

"I heard that too from Lib. I also heard from Mary Lou Knorr's daughter in law Mrs. Puckett has taken off unexpectedly to the Jersey shore with their son." I decided not to verify that little tidbit even though I had seen her earlier. As far as anyone knew, I was just walking my dog when I saw Mrs. Puckett loading the car. I decided to get Lilly off the subject.

"Let me tell you about the worst of the Historical Review Committee."

"What could be worse than what they've already done?"

I told her about the tax credits and the conditions they required. Lilly started sputtering as if she was gnashing her teeth over that. "And to think I can't even put a window in I can afford. Can't afford the higher taxes coming and they don't have to pay taxes for five years!"

"Lilly, now you know why this body was driven to drink before it was even noon."

"I feel like one too. They can't do that! It's gotta be some kind of discrimination!"

"Yes they can and yes they will and yes it is blatant discrimination of the senior citizens of Mountain Empire."

"Tiggy, tell me what I can do and I'll do it."

"O.K. Lilly, one thing we need to find out is if the Christmas open house on Beverley Street and Sherwood Ave is a sure thing. That would sure go a long way to making the Historical Committee rethink these paint requirements. After all, they wouldn't want to put up banners out by the highway to draw paying visitors if they were going to look like fools. I seriously doubt the Historical Committee wants a bunch of polka dot houses on tour, N'est pas?"

"Oh Tiggy, you are a stitch. You know that?"

I told her with Mrs. Puckett out of town, we might be able to enlist Shelby to find out the details for us. Under the guise of participating of course. We could even wrestle control of the open house idea since Beverley and Sherwood area had a tradition of decorating for Christmas. There was no other way to get Shelby to help us unless we feigned friendly interest. The incomers had made her wealthy and she was on their side. Lilly felt better after that and pledged to contact Jimmy Knorr and Doc Wiley for help in organizing our painting protest. We agreed it should happen tout suite in order to have its full effect.

7 DOTTING THE TOWN

It was going to take a lot of perspiration to carry out my inspiration. We were already into the last half of August and our neighborhood block party was looming. It would have been bad form to "dot" the town so to speak, right before a social occasion involving incomers and citizens. Lib was to be kept in the dark no matter what. After all is said and done, blood is thicker than water. The element of surprise was our greatest weapon. If that Nibruska or Hugh McMinn got wind of what we were planning, they might have tried to discourage us. Dear Mrs. Puckett was still not back from the Jersey shore and that gave us a chance to meet at Mary Lou's without being noticed. The house on Central sold and Darla was in the process of divorcing Bobby. She and the girls would be remaining in the house she and Pete had bought together in the first place. Who cares where Bobby landed.

Bill Puckett and Darla had not ever been seen together as far as I knew. Nobody but Pookie and I knew about Bobby pounding on the door that night on Central Avenue. Miss Mary Lou never registered it was Darla walking the black dog down her street as an excuse to be at the vacant house. Whatever reason Darla separated from her second husband was to remain unknown for now. However, if Bill and Darla were really an item, there was no talk of him separating from his wife. As a matter of fact, he told Shelby he had bought a new hot water heater just for his and Spookay Pookay's bathroom. I remembered Pete's delivery truck there a few weeks back. The new hot water heater in the Pucketts turned out to be downright deadly. It just so happened to do its damage when only Bill, the Macau and the mannequin were in the house.

The morning I discovered the whole disaster was a few days after Estelle and I began organizing our paint coup. Pookie and I went out our usual time just before daylight. Bobby's dog was no longer terrorizing us so we took our time. I headed up to Central Ave, curious as ever whether the Pucketts were actually cohabitating. As I approached the crossover from Beverley Street I saw her car was still gone. I noticed the spotlight shining on the mannequin. Then I froze for a moment and took off across the street to the Pucketts like a bat out of you know where. The Macau was lying on his back, feet up in the air. You could see him motionless, eyes closed, on the feeding platform. Pookie began sniffing and barking so franticly I couldn't hear myself think.

I began knocking on the Puckett's door, the windows, and I unlocked their back gate to try that part of the house. I could not rouse a soul. I picked up Pookie and ran across the side street to Mary Lou's. I knew she got up early. She couldn't hear well enough to know I was pounding on her front door. Everybody in town was aware her doorbell didn't work. I ran to her back gate and couldn't open it. I hooked Pookie's leash on the post and climbed her gate. She finally noticed me as I came over the gate; she came to the door looking puzzled. I pushed past her like a whirlwind. In passing I said, "Good morning Mary Lou" and walked straight to the phone. I dialed 911 and gave the Puckett's address and told them to call an ambulance or something because nobody answered the door. Mary Lou stood there with her mouth hanging open.

"Did you say I didn't answer the door?" she asked me in quizzical fashion.

"No, No, Miss Mary Lou, it's your neighbors on the side that wouldn't answer." She rolled her eyes as if to say, is that all? "Oh Tiggy, they are not friendly to anyone."

I told her about the dead bird in the window and beating on the door and windows. She got wide eyed.

"Oh! What in Sam Hill is going on?"

She leaned across a chair and opened the shades to look out her side window.

Then I remembered, "Oh, ye Gods and little catfishes! Pookie is tied to your fence!"

I ran out the back and rescued her. She had practically choked herself pulling the leash across the top of the gate! I was upset enough with the bird dead and no way to know if anyone was in the Puckett's house.

Just then, I heard the rescue squad siren and the fire truck. Holding Pookie, I helped Mrs. Knorr on with a raincoat over her nightgown. Then I went down the back entrance stairs two steps at a time and went across to the Pucketts. The policeman pulled up; it was the one who had been on floor duty when Lilly started her complaint about Hugh McMinn's dog. He had his flashlight in his hand like a weapon and the thing on his belt had voices coming out of it that he answered from his collar.

"Are you the one who called in the alarm?"

"Yes officer, I don't know if the husband has gone out of town or what, but that bird is dead! Dead as a doornail!"

I tried to follow him in and one of the firemen stopped me. A few minutes later they came out with someone on a stretcher. They were gathered around the person trying to shield them. Mary Lou ran back to her house and I could see her on the phone. Lilly walked up with Jenny and Beaucoup and asked me what happened. I didn't answer her for a moment. I asked the rescue guy, "Is it a man or woman? Is it a teenage boy?"

"Ma'am, do you know how many residents there were in this house?" I told him about the wife and son but that they were supposedly at the Jersey shore.

Then he asked me if I knew of any relatives or next of Kin. I didn't know the answer. I told him the only one who might know would be the incomer friends of theirs or maybe their realtor, Shelby Ann Wytheville. The man wrote all of that down but he kept walking. I craned my neck and saw it was Bill; even through the oxygen mask you could see it wasn't the son. Then the firemen came out and told the crowd that had gathered to get back to the sidewalk. One of the incomers was standing by his bike, dressed like a crash dummy. He said, "Everything's fine, the only tragedy is the bird."

As he turned his bike to ride on I couldn't help saying, "Young man, the bird dying is sad but the man could have been killed too. He's not out of the woods yet. In this town we value people first and animals second."

Then I turned on my heel and went over to stand by Lilly. I heard him as he sheepishly said, "Well, I care about people too."

The midday news was all about the whole incident that day. The camera showed a live shot of the Puckett house with the dead bird and mannequin in the window. I was fit to be tied over showing that stupid mannequin. It made Mountain Empire look like a bunch of weirdos. The cause of everything at the Pucketts was a carbon monoxide leak from the hot water heater. The man on the news described the problem as incorrectly made flue gas baffles. "The flue baffles may affect fuel combustion resulting in excessive carbon monoxide emissions. The owners of the property had central air which helped distribute the poison gas throughout the house.

I asked the man on the television, "Well, is Bill Puckett alive or what?"

"Fortunately, there were no deaths resulting from the carbon monoxide poisoning except a family pet. We have called the manufacturer and have been told this model has been recalled for this very reason. We are hereby warning the public to check for the following identification criteria regarding their hot water heater. If you currently have a CPSC-1,220 75 gallon with the following serial numbers:M11TW757T6EN12 or M11TW757T6Cx12 please contact a plumber immediately." Then he gave a web site and a toll free phone number to call for a special kit to change the flue baffles.

I called Carter Crawford and left a message for him to come by for a look at my hot water heater lickety split.

I figured we would need to let this turn of events die down before we would be able to set the wheels in motion on our plans for the polka dots. I heard through Mary Lou Mrs. Puckett didn't get back until the day after her husband got home from the hospital. I took food over to him before she had returned. He was genuinely appreciative for my providential role in saving his life.

"That's what neighbors do for each other."

I wanted to say, "Now you owe me. How about telling your wife to put a sock in it, regarding our Christmas traditions."

My upbringing precluded me from saying it at such a difficult time.

The summer evaporated after that and Lib, Lilly, Estelle and I busied ourselves organizing the pig roast and assigning side dishes to our neighbors for the Labor Day extravaganza. Start time was to be the standard four o'clock to dark thirty. Dark thirty usually came when the food and liquor was consumed. It was Lib's turn to have it. I knew dear Shelby would be there to shmooze with all of her former clients. She never missed a chance to get business now. I was hoping she wouldn't bring Martha Lofton but the two were a team now. It was supposed to be residents of Beverley Street, Ivy Heights and Sherwood area. I assumed that awful daughter of Hugh and Betty's would have the good sense not to come. I was wrong, and right to think she was ill bred. Not only did she come, but made a point to tell me she had given her dog away before she knew it had bitten anyone. She must have thought I was stupid. Then she gave me some song and dance, how if she only knew where the people moved she would have told the authorities. A likely story from a spoiled, yuppie brat. I had visions of the dog sitting in a kennel somewhere at her home in Richmond, waiting for "Mommy Dearest". She seemed more interested in talking about saving trees then anything else. I politely excused myself from her and got a stiff drink. Hugh and Betty were inhaling daiquiris like they were going out of style. Pete Gwaltney brought his girls but Darla didn't show.

The Pucketts came as a family but Mrs. Puckett left after eating. Bill and the son stayed behind and seemed quite congenial. Someone asked Pete if he had installed the hot water heater in the Pucketts. He answered in the affirmative and told us he had to special order that hot water heater at the behest of Mrs. Puckett. Til my dying day, I will believe that woman looked up things on her computer like: dangerous hot water heaters. I wouldn't put it past her to have left town hoping the heater would malfunction. No one had thought to see if there had been any tampering on those baffles that could have expedited the leaks. With Central air, the carbon monoxide must have been recirculating constantly. Mrs. Puckett struck me as the kind of person who could get angry over nothing. Even suspecting her husband was having an affair, to say she could be vindictive is a masterpiece of understatement.

Bill Puckett seemed to be having a good time without his wife there. John and Joanna told Lib in the kitchen they would be glad to stay and make sure the grill was completely out. They didn't drink near as much as the other incomers. I planned to stay to the bitter end and help Lib clean up. Shelby made sure to leave before being tasked. Around ten thirty, Hugh was drunk as a skunk. He and Pete Gwaltney began talking about pranks they did in college while under the influence. John and Joanna were laughing so hard they spewed a drink. I began going around with a garbage bag, picking up stray plastic cups and forks. Hugh McMinn had the small group that remained in rapt attention. From the far end of the yard I noticed he was telling another prank story, quietly and surreptitiously.

All of a sudden the group got quiet, I moved closer to listen. If it was too off color I was sending Hugh packing. He was telling about the time he was in college at the University of Tampa. I didn't catch the name of the school. He described how his fraternity brothers got pledges to help them move a bull dozer from a median to the middle of the road being widened.

"Boy, the next day it was curtains for somebody. The news showed a picture of a car that was smashed like an accordion. They had to be going above the speed limit to hit the dozer with that much force. So, oh well, their mistake."

He said it with all the remorse and warmth of a slab of marble. Then he laughed and downed his drink. Betty McMinn was already passed out on Lib's wrought iron settee. The crowd broke up rather quickly after Hugh's story, to say the least. I went into the Kitchen to ask Lib if she minded if I went home to let Pookie out for a minute. She said not to bother with anything else until tomorrow.

"Next time, we need to set a drink limit. We've never gone this late before."

I agreed with her. I hugged her goodnight and as I left out the side yard, everybody but John and Joanna were gone.

They were busy with the hose, drowning the hot coals. I told them it had been a pleasure seeing them. They seemed very somber and subdued. After the stories from Hugh, I was mortified. I wondered if he was just making things up to look tough. Hugh presented himself as the soul of conscience when it came to protecting the environment. He drove thirty miles each month to recycle their plastic and aluminum. He had even installed a wastewater tank at his truck wash. He claimed ground water needed to be preserved at all costs. Not a mention of his daughter's dog ruining poor Beaucoup. He came off calloused and cold in my book in the way he had told about moving the road equipment. Hugh made it sound as if the poor victims had caused their own wreck. The man's lack of conscience disturbed me.

The next day I went over to help Lib clean up after the party. We discussed the incomers and the food they had contributed. We citizens brought vegetables, salads, and Estelle brought her famous rolls. Lilly brought a red velvet cake, Mary Lou didn't stay but she brought a homemade angel food cake. Her son brought her ice cream machine. It was already clean and waiting outside Lib's front door for whenever he came by. Incomers brought chips, salsa and booze but nothing homemade.

"Well Lib, other than the couple from Mattie's old house, did any other incomers help with the clean up?"

"No, John and Joanna were the only ones. I told them we do not consider them incomers anymore." Then she laughed and told me she had told them they were officially citizens for helping in the cleanup.

"Tiggy, I told Joanna it was grand to have kept most of the original furnishings but for pity sake, go ahead and change the name on the mailbox.

"You know Lib, I had forgotten they still have the name Fisher on the mail box."

"Tiggy, I went ahead and told them we didn't exactly welcome the kind of changes Hugh and Nibruska and the Pucketts were trying to effect. They told me they were all for whatever we decided."

"I'll stop over and fill them in on everything. Hey Lib, do you realize all we know them as are John and Joanna? Let's get their last name before we look like a couple of yahoos."

I made a point to stop by their house as I walked back home from Lib's. They weren't home but I saw a letter poking out of the mail box by the front door. I cocked my head to the side so I could make out Joanna's name on the return address end of the envelope. It said Joanna Blake, so finally we knew their last name. I took a wadded receipt from my purse and wrote my phone number with a note. It said:
Please call me tonight at your convenience.
Your neighbor,
Tiggy Adams

That evening Joanna called and asked me what was up. I explained we were having a meeting at my house the next day. I told her we all hoped she and her husband would come. The next night I had everybody who was anybody over for cake and coffee. We had to firm up our plans and how we were going to execute them. It was a rousing success. I had managed with Estelle and Lilly to organize our friends and neighbors throughout Beverley Street area and all through Ivy Heights to prepare to paint! Jimmy Knorr enlisted the help of his son and the son's friends to paint Estelle's house a drab gray green. The polka dot color planned for the front of Estelle's was going to be a reddish brown. It was going to make it easy and less expensive for all of us to only paint the dots on the front of our houses. Once our mission of polka dots was completed, only the front would have to be repainted. My house had just been painted two years earlier with oil based white. I chose the colonial blue for my dots. Jimmy and his son were going to repaint the front of all our homes for a nominal fee as soon as we felt we had made our statement. Lib was still unaware of what we were planning.

Doc Wiley had eleven homes in Ivy Heights pledged to the cause. Main Street area had fifteen houses agreeing to join us. We each studied our color charts and made the selections for dot color. We chose the most contrasting combinations of color imaginable. The 'authentic' Eastlake homes had a variety of rose and yellow hues from which to choose. To tell you the truth, most of the houses in Main Street area were white or off white. Only Estelle had gotten grief over her desire to keep her house blue. It was the principle of the thing that motivated all of us.

It was Mrs. Pookay/Puckett's snotty quote in the paper that really made the majority of our neighbors willing to participate. We considered it our duty to pull out all the stops when it came to decorating for Christmas. Who cares if we all hung lights on the bushes or put out our faded snowmen and candy canes. We resented any deviation from that tradition more than anything the incomers had tried to do to us. Good Golly, Mary Lou Knorr spent three days each year decorating her yard and home for Christmas. She added something new each year and some of it was tacky, but the children loved it. Her home was a brick Queen Anne, which had been painted a cream for the longest time. She opted for black dots on the front of her home. Her grandson offered to paint the dots all around her home. He promised to power wash the house after the dot days and do a fresh paint job. Since he would be repainting for free, she accepted his offer.

Pete Gwaltney used his computer to print out several banners in bold print. They read, I SUPPORT THE DOTS AND CHRISTMAS LIKE IT WAS. We already had a list of people to give those to. They were to be posted in store fronts, on cars, in front windows, etc. I added Mr. Dipendrah and Mr. Panisandra to that list. I purposely left the Panisandras out of the loop for painting dots. I was afraid if we got them to paint dots on their house, they might just leave them. As nice a family as they were, they had atrocious taste. I wouldn't have put it past them to leave dots on their house for all eternity. Gopal might serve our cause more effectively by putting the banner in his front window. Maybe I would get Pete to leave off the part about Christmas for Krishna and Gopal. For all I knew, they might be card carrying Methodists but I didn't have time to find out.

It had been a few weeks since all the hooplah about Darla and Bill Puckett had come out. Estelle was so busy helping plan our coup de tat, the subject hadn't come up. I kept expecting her to bring it up a thousand times but she didn't. Late one night, after all my lights down stairs were off, she showed up. It was when I least expected to see anyone which is why I had caked green mask on my face. She knocked on my front door and Pookie barked once. Then she wagged her tail at the door. I knew from that, it was a friend.

"Who is it?"

"Tiggy, it's me, Estelle." From her tone of voice I knew it wasn't a social call so I let her in out of concern.

"Pete is beside himself over Darla. With Bobby out of the picture, she still refuses to discuss anything about reconciliation."

I don't know if I had been Darla, I would have wanted to discuss my husband leaving after he found out I was having an affair. Particularly with the man I had divorced for another man.

"Now 'Stelle, Darla is probably ashamed, don't you think?" "No Tiggy, Pete has tried numerous times to get back together with her since Bobby moved out. She accused him of boring her to death"

I just listened because there was no good answer.

"Tiggy, he has told her over and over he forgives her. Reverend Stevens told Pete he was at the ready to counsel them. Why Tiggy, Pete is still so in love with Darla and those girls. He's even making a lot more money with the new appliances he's selling. He has a whole line of what they call, retro view. He says these new appliances are made to look like old ones. Apparently they are selling like hot cakes. He's even got a website and customers have come from as far away as Lexington." I thought to myself, I'm not so sure I'd ever buy a new hot water heater again from anybody.

I never thought Pete could be as industrious with the appliance business as he had turned out to be. Maybe the hard times had inspired him to make more of himself. Estelle droned on and on about what Pete wanted. I liked Pete, but not enough to stand in my kitchen at eleven P.M., with green mask on my face, listening to his mother talk about his love life. I told Estelle to go home and say a prayer for the situation.

"I'm sorry but tomorrow those teenage boys are starting all our paint jobs remember?"

"Oh yes, I think we are doing the right thing don't you Tiggy?"

"Absolutely, categorically, unequivicably, definitely, do I make my point Estelle?" She laughed and forgot her troubles. "Tiggy, what do you think that Historical group is gonna say when this all happens tomorrow?"

"The objective is not to have them do anything but shut up!"

8 WAR PAINT

The next morning must have appeared normal to the incomers. Every citizen involved in the polka dot protest was up early setting out drop cloths and what not. Many had hired the Tuition Painters and there were a slew of them arriving by seven A.M. Jimmy Knorr's family and friends were sitting in Mary Lou's yard, poised to begin. There's no doubt in my mind, the incomers saw all those fixit trucks and vans and thought nothing of it. Incomers had been in a constant state of remodeling, landscaping and painting for the last few years. They were pointing at the tarps and equipment being laid out on the lawns. I watched them nodding smugly as I passed them on my morning constitution with Pookie. It was the usual crowd of joggers and bikers dressed like crash test dummies. I could just imagine them assuming we were finally falling into line and following their lead.

It was decided beforehand not to ready, aim and paint until eight fifteen that morning. Incomers did their running or biking before daylight. They would be on their way to "work" by seven-forty five A.M. and none the wiser. Jimmy told me the dots could easily be done in an hour with his homemade stamp. He made one for everybody by tracing a garbage can lid on a large piece of carpet pad. Then he took two-sided carpet tape to secure the stamp inside each garbage lid. It was an ingenious idea worthy of praise from all of us paying painters by the hour. Necessity is the mother of invention. Forget Historic Preservation, we seniors were interested in self-preservation. Jimmy's stamp idea was sure to make the whole process quick, easy, and less expensive.

I had barely slept the night before and suspect many of us involved in the project were running on nervous energy. Estelle's house had been power washed the week before. Due to a lazy, good for nothing painter, her home was not primed and painted the day after the power wash. She was fit to be tied when her painter wouldn't even return her call. Her home was the only one in real need of a complete new paint job. Jimmy Knorr and his son and nephew had personally primed and painted her house the week before we all did our dots. They charged her for the paint, plus twelve dollars an hour. They worked like dogs to finish on time for our big day. It was gratifying to see neighbor helping neighbor like we used to.

Lilly and Estelle went to every person and business sympathetic to our cause with the banners. John and Joanna were agreeable to a banner on the front gate of their house. Around eleven A.M., I walked up and down Beverley and Central and halfway to First Street taking lunch orders. I had bought enough bread, tuna and ham to make sandwiches for a small army. The student painters were in the dark as to what was going on until Mary Lou gave them the details. Some of the kids were students of Hugh McMinn's and worked at his truck wash. As it turns out, Hugh wasn't very popular with them. It's safe to say those of his students working on the dots were inspired to work fast and furiously. Just before I set out to drop off the sack lunches, Lib pulled out of her driveway. She was headed to get her hair color touched up with Blonde # 3. The beautician told her she should go lighter than her natural color when she first started going gray. Unfortunately, Lib believed her over me. Lib stopped her car at the corner where I was crossing.

"Tiggy, since when does everybody in God's creation paint their house on the same day?"

I didn't want to lie but I was not going to volunteer the facts. "Lib, everybody isn't painting today, it just looks like it."

She gave me the strangest look as she rotated her head from front to side to side, looking at the buzz of people in half the yards on our street. There was so much noise and so many people working on houses it looked like the seventeen year cicadas had returned after ten years instead of the usual seventeen. People were indeed everywhere. Radios were blasting from every direction with gosh awful teen age music.

Lib said, "I know you're up to something Tiggy. I can smell it; I've known you too long." I just smiled.

"I wish I had time to chat but maybe this evening, O.K.?" Lib rolled her eyes like she knew we would most certainly have something to talk about.

"O.*K*...... later. Definitely."

As she drove down Main, she lurched and half stopped several times. The dots were obvious and yet they could have been misconstrued as test swatches. I knew she would get to the beauty shop and tell everybody and their brother what she had seen. Heck fire, the beauty shop had one of our banners. She didn't even ask me why I was carrying fifty leven paper lunch bags. She was too busy gawking. I walked briskly to deliver the lunches. Everything was in place and it wouldn't be long before the "cat" and the tuna sandwiches were out of the bag.

Mary Lou had a bunch of plastic milk jugs made up with sweet tea or water. I went from site to site and hollered at the student painters to go to 305 Central for something to drink. Then I went back to the house and let Pookie out on her leash. I was about to head over to Ivy Heights with some lunch for the kids painting over there. The phone was ringing and I saw the message light flashing with messages. I didn't have time to dawdle so I waved the phone ringing away and headed out. As I drove through the old stucco entrance to Ivy Heights, I was awestruck at the sight. Doc Wiley and the other Ivy Heights citizens with Tudor homes had painted big and little dots on their front doors. The Ivy Heights citizens with brick bungalows had done the same. I could understand fully why they only painted their front doors. What's more, they had all gone in together to buy the paint. Every door had dots painted in the same yellow gold. It was absolutely hysterical to see the cars slowing down and people pointing.

I pulled up at Doc's and he came from his neighbor's yard to speak to me.

"I've got y'all some lunch and sweet tea Doc. By the way, how did y'all make your dots in different sizes?"

I didn't get out of the car so he leaned in my driver's window. He lifted a piece of news paper with various circles cut out of it.

"We traced the lids off mayonnaise jars on the newspaper, cut them out and taped the stencil to the door."

Then he pointed to some smaller circles on the paper he was holding and said, "These are from the lid off a jar of olives." Then he laughed.

"Tiggy, I gotta hand it to you. If this doesn't wake some folks up to what we will and will not put up with, nothin' is."

"Doc, we're just takin a page from the sixties, when some of these ranchers were built. This is an act of civil disobedience!"

He started laughing so hard he couldn't talk. His son was one of the very ones who protested the Viet Nam war and was now sympathetic to the Historical Committee.

I chatted a few more minutes with Doc Wiley and then headed back towards Sherwood. I waved at the citizens of Ivy Heights who were sitting on their front porches as I drove away. Just as I was leaving, Woody and some other council member were driving into Ivy Heights. They were talking so intently to each other they didn't even notice me until I had already passed. I turned on the radio to the oldies station and James Taylor was singing the song: Steam Roller. I sang it with new found energy. As I drove down Beverley, the cars were stopping and the people in them were looking right to left and back again. I noticed a van with the local television channel letters on it. No one was in the van and I didn't see any reporter I might recognize. I went into the alley and parked in my garage.

I could hear Pookie barking to beat the band inside. I opened the door and as I put my keys and purse on the kitchen table I saw Pookie lunging at the front door. She looked like she had St. Vitas Dance. I saw my message light on my phone flashing like crazy. I went to the door and picked up Pookie and peeked through the safety hole in the door. I didn't recognize the two men.

"Yes, who is it?"

"We're from WSVA, may we talk to you for a moment? It's about your protest against the city."

I swung open the door and put on my best smile.

"Why Gentlemen, whatever gave you the idea we were protesting the city?"

The well-dressed one said, "Well Ma'am, suppose you tell us what these polka dots are all about." I stepped out on the porch and offered them a seat.

"We who are citizens of the newly designated Historic Districts are simply following the strict painting code devised by the Historical Review Committee of incomers, that is all." Then the man turned on his microphone and the ratty looking man stood up and turned his camera on me. I introduced myself and asked the man his name. He awkwardly shook my hand and said his name was David.

"Now, Mrs. Adams, you spoke earlier about citizens and incomers. Exactly what do you mean? What is the difference between a citizen or an incomer?" I could hear the March to Aida in my head as I sat up in my chair.

"You see David, those of us who have lived here in Mountain Empire for generations or have a history here are citizens. We have existed happily with zoning laws to establish the well-kept look of our town. When we began getting so many new people in here paying high prices for our vacant homes, they saw fit to register this neighborhood as a historic district. This would have all been well and fine. What the incoming people or incomers did, was go a step too far by forming a Historical Review Committee. This committee passed over zealous architectural covenants regarding our property, behind our back. They greedily voted property tax exemptions for themselves too. Part of those underhanded, illegal, property restrictions can dictate what colors we can paint, the cost and type of windows we can replace.

Presently, Historical Review Committee members are trying to insert rules restricting our Christmas decorations. They have been quoted in our local paper as wanting only those decorations that are in conjunction with the year each house was built."

I was about to continue, when my student painter came from working across the street.

She was ready to be paid and head back to Mountain Laurel College. I said excuse me to David and went inside to get my purse. Before I could give the man a chance at her, I motioned her inside. She followed me to the kitchen and I wrote her a check. I escorted her to the front door and went out on the porch to finish the interview, but the man was half way down the street. He had left me his business card with a note that said, "Please call me."

Mr. David "the bad" mannered reporter, was talking into his microphone as he walked. The camera man who looked like something off a wanted poster, was filming. I ran inside and called everybody I could to advise them to send David the television man back to me with any questions. I spoke personally to Lilly and Doc; left a message on Estelle's phone and told Miss Mary Lou to call everybody on Central and give them the same instructions. I wasn't about to let the television people twist our words. I was about to retrieve my phone messages when the phone rang. It was a participant over in Ivy Heights. She told me her husband had warned everybody to get inside and not answer the door. I thanked her kindly and we hung up. It was just after noon, the fertilizer was about to hit the fan.

I pushed the playback button on my answering machine. Lilly was first….

"Tiggy, should I let these painters play their radio? Won't that bring too much attention to everything?"

I talked back to the phone as the next message was playing. "Lilly, the polka dots are gonna be more obvious then the radio dear!"

I had to rewind the machine. I got through Lilly again and Mrs. Spookay Pookay said, "Tiggy, could you please call me. I understand you have some input regarding the Christmas Open House and walking tour."

"I think you have already received my input dear!"

The next messages were from various and sundry neighbors, asking me the dumbest questions.

I was about to get Pookie on the leash for a "walking tour" as Mrs. Puckett would have termed it when the front doorbell rang twice. Pookie ran to the door, barked once and then sniffed. Her tail wasn't wagging though. I went to the door and peered through the peephole. It was Lib Wytheville, her hair newly blondeened and sprayed into the shape of Darth Vader's helmet. Standing next to her was dear Shelby Ann. I opened the door.

"Hey, come on in y'all!"

Lib had an expression on her face like she was auditioning for a headache commercial. Shelby Ann's demeanor was so stiff you'd have thought she was wearing a neck brace. The two of them spoke at the same time. Both smiled with a weak greeting of "Hey." Then Shelby opened her big mouth. "Miss Tiggy, what is going on?"

"You mean our polka dots?"

"Hello! Yes I mean the polka dots!"

"What would you like to know about them?" Then she acted all wounded.

"Miz Adams, I was showing clients around a little while ago. They got out of my car and walked up to someone at Mrs. Knorr's and practically got their head bit off for asking a simple question."

"Don't you remember how those other clients of yours started the historical covenants and tried to bankrupt her over a new roof?"

She looked down at her three hundred dollar shoes.

"I just don't remember things like that for any length of time. Life has to go on, you know."

Lib said, "What she means Tiggy is…"

To which I replied with vinegar behind every drop of sugar, "Why Lib honey, Shelby is expressing herself very well."

Lib sat down on my living room sofa and Shelby stayed leaning against the entry. She was ready to make a hasty retreat.

"It's just, well………………………, I have to make a living and the situation today blew a mega deal for me."

"Aw Shelby, if you would get these Historical covenants lifted from those of us who are longtime citizens, you would be the hero of the day. At least tell that Mrs. Puckett, her meddling into our Christmas decorating is what motivated the majority of polka dots you have seen today."

Lib said, "Shell, you know I have always draped red and white lights on both sides of my boxwoods. It's been that way since your mama was knee high to a grasshopper. The incomers have gone a little too far. Frankly, they are just plain overbearing."

"Grandmama, that's the way things are done in the bigger cities. They don't mean anything by it!"

I said as gently as I could, "Shelby, they moved into our territory we didn't move into theirs. They have ready cash to make improvements on their homes which allow them a five year rebate on property taxes. Now the older citizens have to pay higher taxes and they pay nothing for five years."

Lib's eyes got big as saucers.

"Tiggy, what in the name of my favorite black dress are you talking about?"

I told her to wait a sec, then I produced the literature Mr. Creel had given me. I opened it to the page about the tax credits.

"Read it and weep." Shelby came and read over Lib's shoulder. She got as quiet as a church mouse, reading with her grandmother. In a few minutes Lib turned to Shelby and said, "Shelby Ann! I am going home to paint dots on my house too! Why I never!"

"Y'all can't get away with this. The city is gonna make you clean it up."

"No Shelby, we are completely within our rights and within the covenants. In order to disallow the dots it would have to be voted on by every voter. I've got news for you sweetheart, the majority of citizens are on our side. It's time to play by our rules if there is going to be a Christmas tour!" The next thing I heard from Lib was, "That's right! I'm your grandmother! The one whose house you hope to inherit some day! You better talk to those people you sold houses to!" Shelby stuck her bottom lip out so far she almost stepped on it.

"Grand, please don't you join in. I'll talk to Hugh McMinn and Bill Nibruska. How about that?"

Lib and I both said, "Good. That's our girl!" Then Lib and Shelby both stood up and walked towards the front door.

I walked them out to the porch and surveyed the street. The dodgy looking camera man and David were leaned against their van. "I advise you not to give them any information, good or bad." Lib said, "Say no more, done!"

I watched both of them drive away and noticed it was almost three in the afternoon. Soon Hugh McMinn, and Mrs. Puckett's son would drive down Beverley and Central. I could hear the phone ringing and thought: boy am I popular today!

I answered the phone: "Grand Central Station, Tiggy speaking." It was Hazel calling.

"Well Tiggy, I haven't had a minute today."

"Tell me about it!"

"I'm gonna have to re-order coffee. I normally don't sell this much unless it's the night of the Christmas parade. Guess what?"

"No games Hazel, I'm all tuckered out."

"Well, I'm gonna be on T.V. tonight! The guys from TV were here for a long time. They asked me about the Historical Review Committee and the incomers and everything."

"Well Hazel, looks like your old friends and neighbors are good for business."

"Y'all sure have been, and I don't mean maybe."

"Pookie is in desperate need of a walk so I can't jaw any longer.

"O.K., I won't keep you Tiggy, but thank YEW." I told her I was happy to help an old friend and then we hung up. The phone rang before I could get Pookie's leash on. "Come on Pookie, let's get while the getting's good."

When we passed Mattie's old house, I noticed John and Joanna had finally put their name on the mail box. Right below

Mattie's glow in the dark, stick on letters spelling Fisher, were scripted letters that said Blake. I was touched by their nostalgia. Part of their house would always be the Fisher place to me. I said it to myself, Fisher-Blake, what a lovely gesture of John and Joanna. I noticed more strange people riding slowly up and down the street as I walked. Hugh McMinn's fancy Volvo wasn't in the driveway. When I got to the crossover to Central, Mrs. Puckett was at her front window. She was adjusting a change of clothes on her mannequin/Victorian Voodoo doll. I had hardly reached the sidewalk before Mary Lou came to the door and waved me over. Her black dots were only on the front after all. It still had the desired effect.

"Looks good Mary Lou."

"Tiggy, Woody already called me and asked me to ask you if we would allow the city to come and repaint over the dots. I told him we had a lot of new concerns to discuss concerning the historic rules and you know who's ideas about Christmas." She cast her head towards the Pucketts when she said that.

"Has Mrs. Pookay said anything to you?"

Mary Lou said that so far she was being very solicitous. I told her I wasn't surprised. Having to look at the polka dots right next to their house would teach her a lesson.

"I haven't forgotten the mean way she treated me when I was going through that mess with my roof."

"Mary Lou, stay polite but stay strong. Let the dots do the talking." She told me she was almost eighty three and had nothing to lose by waiting- - unless it was for a new roof. Then we both laughed and I continued on home. The phone was ringing as I came in the door. I had to have a nap before dealing with anyone else. I played the messages back and turned the phone off. I had a message from Betty McMinn, Bill Nibruska and the guy from the television station. They were all asking me to call them. How many times had I tried to talk to them and they avoided me. Too many times to count and I was so tired, I was down for the count. Pookie and I headed upstairs for a nap.

I fell so fast asleep I couldn't have even counted backwards from ten. I woke up at five thirty that afternoon to someone leaning on my doorbell. I hollered out the front window, "I'm coming!" Pookie hadn't barked at all and still acted calmly. I peeped through the door and opened it. It was Lilly, Estelle and Lib. My hair was all flat on one side. Estelle asked me how long I'd been asleep and I looked at my living room clock.

"About an hour and a half, why?"

Lilly said, "Well, you're gonna have your fifteen minutes of fame just like the rest of us. We wanna go to the Lick Skillet and eat supper. We can get Hazel to put the T.V. on."

I told them to let me get my lipstick and pearls on and change into dress slacks. I still wasn't sure Lib was totally on our side. She soon put me at rest as we walked to her car. While she drove, she confided how Lilly and Estelle had told her everything they had gone through with incomer's dogs. She chided us,

"We've been through wars, childbirth, retired husbands, and murder in our hearts over those husbands. Friendship got us through it all. We will go through this together too. Shelby's pocketbook be damned, she's got too many of them anyway."

We all patted her on the back with a "That's our Lib". As we parked in front of the Lick Skillet, the banner was front and center on the door. I pointed to the banner and said, "All together now…………." We all said in unison as we got out of the car: "I support the polka dots and Christmas like it was!"

9 DEATH AND TAXES

Lib had made sure to call Hazel before showing up at my house with Lilly and Estelle. Hazel was kind enough to reserve four seats at the counter, so we could have the best view of the television. I spied salt and pepper shakers sitting in the seats saved for us. I didn't even have to ask whether or not those were our places. Lib had forgotten to mention calling Hazel until we got inside. I knew if any places were spoken for, they were for us. The television was already on, and the six o'clock news was just about to start. We sat down and Hazel hollered through the cut out in the kitchen.

"I see y'all found your places."

There were so many people in the Lick Skillet, you couldn't have stirred them with a stick.

We had to sit through the national headlines first. Finally, that dumb David fellow came on the screen. He was standing right in front of Mary Lou's. Wouldn't you know, he introduced the story as a citizen's revolt against the Historical Review

Committee and City Council. As the camera panned the front of Mary Lou's, it then moved to the side. The next scene on camera was of the Victorian Voodoo doll of Spookay Pookay's.

Hazel said, "Why would somebody put a mannequin in their front window dressed in old fashioned clothes like that?"

"It's a mannequin, slash Victorian voodoo doll!" Everybody in earshot started laughing. The next scene was the interview with Hazel.

"Here it is, that's me, that's my place!"

We were mesmerized listening to Hazel. She explained how the protest started because of her longtime friend Estelle Gwaltney. Hazel mentioned the approved color list for Prairie style homes. Then she expressed resentment as to why Estelle couldn't repaint her house the same color it had been for years.

Estelle said, "Tell it Hazel, tell it like it is."

The interview was cut short and switched to my front porch. I wish I'd had my lipstick on fresh. That dumb David didn't have all my comments and half of what I'd said wasn't played. The camera kept switching from house to house on Main and then to Ivy Heights. Finally it switched back to Dumb David and me on my front porch. The dummie said, "Here with me, is the organizer of the civil disobedience, Mrs. Tilly Adams."

I shouted at the T.V., "Tiggy, not Tilly, can't you get anything right?"

I finally got to explain myself on camera towards the end of the segment. I gave all the reasons we were fed up with the

Historical Review Committee. The last item he had on us was a surprise. He had gotten the list of covenants and mentioned the tax credits for renovation of property in a designated historic district. At long last, he brought up the proposed changes for Christmas decorations in Main Street area. He also said, "As for the garish polka dots you see here, there is no prohibition on how citizens may use approved colors on their houses. The citizens of Mountain Empire are completely within their rights."

All of us qualified as citizens nodded in the affirmative. Then the parting visual was of Mr. Dipendra. He was standing beside his "I support the Polka Dots" banner with a big smile on his face. Then David said, "It looks like one incomer is going to be a citizen of Mountain Empire after today."

Everybody in the Lick Skillet clapped and yelled, "Yay Mr. Dipendra!"

When the news switched to an advertisement, everybody started talking at once, you couldn't hear yourself think. One man,(a citizen) came over to me and asked what the tax credits were all about. He was hoppin' mad about that. I told him the next city council meeting would probably be about the new Christmas decoration guidelines. I suggested he come and bring a petition of names in favor of amending the tax credit. I explained how the petition would influence council to vote fair limits for tax rebates on historic property. Another citizen came up to listen in on us and he asked me if I would consider running for city council. I told him it was definitely food for thought.

As we were chatting, Lamarr Hunt, our mayor, came in with his wife and grandchildren. The buzz of voices lowered a level and all eyes were cast suspiciously at Lamarr. He made a beeline over to me, Estelle, Lilly and Lib.

"Hello ladies, he said. What's good tonight?"

I smiled graciously at him. "Hey Lamarr, hey Callie."

They stood there looking around because there was no table open. All the counter seats were taken too. Hazel said, "It'll be a little while, would you like take out?" Lamarr and Callie took another look around at the stoic looking crowd staring ever so discreetly at them.

Callie said, "Lamarr, let's try the Pickle Barrel." They said goodbye to us at the counter and left.

Hazel said, "I always thought Lamarr was a good person, but he could have stopped those Historical rules from getting out of hand."

Lilly said, "You've got that right."

I reminded everybody present, "Do you think any of our council members would be in favor of anything they didn't profit from?"

Lib said, "His son-in-law owns a small construction company. I happen to know, Martha Lofton has referred a lot of incomers to him. Shelby Ann has Bobby Tatum's card and Carter Crawford's on her office bulletin board. The mayor and the others who have profited from all the incomers owe it all to Shelby Ann and Martha, if you ask me." None of us wanted to touch that comment with a ten foot pole.

Estelle said, "Pete has a web site that has brought him a lot of business. Did y'all know he stocks what is called the retro look? They're appliances that look like the 1920's up to the 1950's." I thought she had told everybody about that by now.

We finished our hamburgers and paid Hazel. As I stood up from the counter with Lib and the gals, applause erupted. It was as thrilling as being crowned Miss America. I left the Lick Skillet feeling ten years younger with seventy years of wisdom. Lib dropped of Estelle and Lilly first. As we were headed back to my house, Lib said, "Tiggy, I've got to tell you something." She sounded serious so I suggested she come in.

"How about I just pull up and park in front for a minute." Then Lib began to tell me the sordid news. It seems Shelby Ann had walked in on Darla and Bill Puckett. Lib said Shelby had two clients with her when Bill and Darla were caught in the act, if you know what I mean. Shelby happened in on them in the middle of the day no less, at the house on Central Ave.

Shelby also told Lib that Darla was involved with Bill Nibruska before she got mixed up with Bill Puckett.

"Lib, have you noticed where Darla goes, disaster follows? Just think about it for a minute. First she leaves Pete for Bobby and Pete is devastated. Bobby practically breaks his neck slipping on a rug. Then, she gets involved with that Nibruska fellow and his house burns to the ground due to the faulty fans. Next, she's with Bill Puckett and he almost dies of affixation."

Lib said, "Aren't you glad you don't live any closer to her than you do?"

"I realize there's a logical explanation for everything but that girl has a cloud over her!"

We sat there in thought for a minute and I said, "Well, it's time to let Pookie out and face my answering machine."

Lib asked me if I had done nothing but answer the phone all day. I laughed at that as I got out of the car and told her goodnight.

Pookie was beside herself waiting for me to take her out. I was too tired to do anything at that point but let her out in the back yard. If she stepped on any of my flowers, so be it. What else was a fence for? I let her out and she ran back and forth at the back of the fence, barking her head off. I turned on the back lights and looked through the sliding door. It was probably a cat or something. I pressed the answering machine and listened. I erased all the messages I'd heard until the last two. One was from Woody asking me to call no matter how late and the other was from Estelle. "Tiggy, I know you're there by now. Call me! Please!"

I called her and she answered on the first ring. She wanted to tell me something Hugh McMinn had done to Pete. I foolishly thought it was going to be something about the day's events or I wouldn't have called back. Hugh had been giving incomers the factory website for the retro appliances and this was cutting into Pete's business. Then she got my attention with the next tidbit.

"Darla is more than friends with Hugh McMinn."

"Estelle, how do you know that?"

"Pete said the girls told him Hugh drops by frequently, and you know she had a thing with Bill Puckett before that? I didn't want to tell you 'cause I thought she and Pete were going to work things out."

I thought to myself, "Everybody in town but you knew that one.

"Estelle, just because Hugh played a dirty trick on Pete doesn't mean his visits to Darla's are anything untoward." "Darla is wilder than you think. You know why she won't get back together with Pete? She told him that he was too much of a goody two shoes. She said he was as exciting as a wet noodle!"

"Estelle, the girl is from a rich family who gave her what she wanted when she wanted. Now that her mother has remarried and has someone else to spend the money on, she's probably getting her kicks another way. She could also be going through some kind of midlife crisis."

"Our generation didn't do things like that, Tiggy."

"I know Estelle, but isn't that why they call us the greatest generation?"

I told her I had to let Pookie in because she wouldn't stop barking. I hung up and let Pookie in and turned out the lights. I decided to close all the first floor windows. September was almost gone but the nights were cool by nine.

I decided to baby gate Pookie in the kitchen that night so I could sleep late the next morning. I was just plain physically and emotionally exhausted. Even though it wasn't completely dark outside, I knew I would go to sleep the minute my head hit the pillow. Around eleven P.M., I heard a noise like someone was slapping something. I thought I was dreaming and Pookie was quiet. I started to doze off when I heard it again. This time I went to my bathroom to look out the window. I saw someone behind Darla's, hitting a car with some kind of stick. It was a long, boxy looking car but without light, I couldn't make out what the car was or if a man or woman was hitting the car.

I yelled out, "See here, this is a good neighborhood. I'm calling the police!"

They took off running and I decided to call Darla. I switched on the light and instead of Darla's, I called the police and told them which alley to come to. Then I called Darla and told her the police were on their way. She didn't even thank me, she just said, "O.K." and hung up. Two seconds later, I heard somebody start the car that had been pounded. They drove away without turning on their headlights.

I had to let Pookie out because she was energized from the commotion. I turned on my back floodlight and let her out and locked the door back. I was too afraid to stand there with the door open after what I had just seen. I thought back to my conversation with Lib earlier. Darla equals trouble any way you looked at it. Bobby Tatum was from a trashy family; the kind of ignorant people who would have no social standards of behavior. He could be out there with a weapon or something. I peeped out the sliding doors, and feeling safe, I opened the door to let Pookie back in. I locked the door back and left my flood light on. Then I switched the front lights on as I headed upstairs. This time I took Pookie up with me and decided to take a dose of cold medicine so I would fall asleep. I peered out the window before getting back into bed. Darla's back lights were on and I could see her talking to the police. She had a shiny robe on and no shoes. I stood there with my bathroom light off so they couldn't see me. The last thing I wanted to do was talk to a cop. I had talked to neighbors, television people, painters and friends. I was talked out and tuckered out. Within minutes, the police drove slowly away, shining their flashlights all down the alley. All I could think was, "Brilliant, the vandal is still in the alley. He's wearing a ski mask and carrying a baseball bat just so you don't miss him." Police do things just to look busy half the time, that's what I think.

The next morning was Friday, probably the busiest time of the week. City council was due to meet Monday and I needed to call everybody I could to remind them to be there. I put on my walking shoes and headed out with Pookie. I peered slowly out my back gate as I opened it. There was no sign of glass or debris behind Darla's. We headed out of the alley and around the front. It was too dark to see the polka dots. I would have thought everybody and their brother would be out. We were the only ones out until I spied Lilly walking Jenny and Beaucoup. I picked Pookie up before she could turn on her barking tape. I chatted with Lilly and mentioned her leg looked fine. She bemoaned the fact she had no reason to go to dog shows this fall. I told her we needed to bring the pictures again of her and Beaucoup's injuries to council meeting Monday night. She said she would call our cohorts in Ivy Heights and remind them about the meeting. I wished her a good day and hurried Pookie up. I knew the morning paper should be on my doorstep by now. I wanted to read the latest on our "dotting".

As I got to the crossover at Main and Central, I noticed the Victorian Voodoo doll was not lit. That meant the Pucketts were up at the regular time. Somebody needed to take note of everyone's daily routine or we wouldn't be a neighborhood. I didn't cross the street at Central. Pookie and I headed back down Beverley towards home. I picked up the paper and started inside, when I noticed something odd at the McMinn's. Hugh's big Volvo station wagon had a huge, round crack in the middle of the front windshield. It looked like a big bull's eye. Could it be Estelle was right about Darla and Hugh? Who would do a thing like that? Certainly no citizen of ours, unless Bobby had wind of something. Bobby was from the most backward part of the county. He was not a Mountain Empire citizen. I had heard he and Darla were already in the process of divorce. All I wanted to think about right now was my first cup of coffee and my morning paper. As I started the coffee, I glanced at the front page headline. It read, LOCAL WOMEN ORGANIZE PROTEST.

If that didn't beat all! It was me, myself and I, who did the organizing. There were quotes in the lead article from my television interview. Hazel, Jimmy Knorr and Mrs. Puckett were all quoted too. The reporter had spelled Mrs. Puckett's last name as: Pooky. I'd bet my life, Mrs.

Puckett had forced the wrong pronunciation of her name. They couldn't even get the wrong name right. Well, at least my name was spelled Tiggy instead of Tilly. Mrs. "Spooky,Pooky" Puckett was asked by the reporter how she felt about the dots. She said it was news to her that anybody was against the color charts or her ideas for period holiday decorations.

Mrs. Puckett went on to say that several people had called her on the telephone in favor of a historically accurate display of holiday decorations.

"You mean everybody on the Historical Committee called you. And quit saying holiday this and holiday that. It's Christmas decorations you blood sucker!"

She came off like Marie Antoinette in the piece. Hugh McMinn was interviewed as was Bill Nibruska. They made an appeal for dialogue with the longtime residents. Nibruska said they wanted to explain how tourism from the Christmas Open house would benefit the town. I was sick and tired of them trying to appear helpful. They never talk to us about anything unless they're forced.

The phone rang and it was Woody.

"Tiggy, are you feeling alright today?"

"Woody I have no complaints."

"Well that's good. Say Tiggy, how about you let me know what I can do to make uhh, to uhh, encourage y'all to take down the banners and repaint y'all's houses right."

"Woody, don't let the "Pooky" woman (and he laughed at that) have any say so in what kind of Christmas decorations we do here and we might be willing. There are many of us who want that five year tax rebate y'all are giving for historic property to be changed to one year, too. We are serious as a heart attack about that. We want to be on the docket at council meeting Monday. The alternative, Woody, means the property values decrease if we have to keep our houses painted like this a year."

"But Tiggy, you can't leave them like they are for a year!" I told him to check the very covenants he had signed into city ordinances. There was a pregnant pause and he acknowledged defeat in his voice.

"Alright, y'all want on the docket, consider it done."

"Then we may just have a solution to the whole mess."

"That's what I want. I want the hard feelings gone."

Then I told him I was coming to the meeting Monday and I expected him to muzzle Mrs. Puckett. He assured me he would.

I felt relieved Woody had treated me like I was used to being treated. I called Estelle and told her about Woody's call.

"That's wonderful Tiggy, isn't that what we wanted?"

I told her it was, but I would believe it when Woody announced it publicly. Then Estelle told me she wanted to go the council meeting to ask again for a traffic light at the end of the town road. It was the one that connected from town to the highway exit and state road. I asked her what brought about her interest. She had almost had a wreck that morning, just like me and so many others at that intersection. Hugh McMinn's truck wash customers had made it ten times worse than it had ever been. I asked Estelle if a big truck had come out of the truck wash at the blind turn where town road to state road intersected.

"Yes Tiggy, has that ever happened to you?"

I reminded her for the umpteenth time, "Yes, and to Lib, Mrs. Reverend Stevens, Lilly, Hazel, why just about everybody!" Then I told her if we just had our old grocery store uptown, we wouldn't even have to use the All Mart. Estelle asked me if I thought it was time to go to winter white. I told her it was, even though it was still hot.

"Estelle, let the fashionable wear white after Labor Day. We are the classics. Why Estelle, you and I and Lilly and Lib are the classics four."

"Should we make up a secret handshake and start a membership drive?"

We both practically laid an egg, laughing at ourselves. I had to get off the phone or I wouldn't get a thing done that day.

I was just about to head upstairs and dress when the doorbell rang. Pookie was at the front door barking in a split second. She started growling so I grabbed her up and peeked through the peep hole. It was Mrs. Puckett, carrying a tray with a cloth over it. I thought it could be someone's head on a platter or a nice dish of arsenic with a side of casserole. I put Pookie down and cracked the door. I squeezed through the door.

"Please have a seat on the porch, I wouldn't want my dog to frighten you. I was thinking all along, "Don't worry Pookie, I won't let the lady eat you."

She jumped in with, "I made these muffins just for you. I want you to know that I value your suggestions to leave Main Street holiday decorations at status quo. Please, let's pretend I never suggested anything about altering your traditions."

I couldn't help but be suspicious as to her true motivation. I thanked her for the muffins even though there wasn't a snowball's chance in hell I would eat them. Then she made a comment about how she admired my feminist spirit. How if she ever wanted to organize community involvement she must use me as her role model. Blah, blah, muckity, muckity, muck. Then she cocked her head in coquettish fashion.

"What would you like me to do for you, so Mrs. Knorr and the rest of the protesters would paint their houses back more attractively?"

Ah ha! Now the truth comes out from the woman with no soul. I looked her straight in the eyes.

"Why, It's not necessary for you to do a thing for me, Mrs. Puckett. Respecting our neighborhood and the people who created it are thanks enough."

She gave me a wan smile and asked, "Well, you do know we are planning the flyers for the publicity surrounding our Christmas tour of homes very soon."

"Then we had better get the ball rolling. Do try to inform new residents about the leash laws—it is a sore point with me. I also believe, there should be variances for citizens who never had the words historic district on their deed. I am also concerned with other issues involving parity in the tax credits for historic property."

The woman began displaying a tick in her left eye. Then I just stared her down with a smile. With her eye twitching and her voice suddenly down in her throat, she got up.

"Any expediting of the situation with the polka dots will be music to my ears."

I told her to have a great day and thanked her again for the lovely muffins. Buffalo muffins, I thought. I went inside, locked the door and put the muffins down the garbage disposal. I did it wearing rubber gloves. Mrs. Puckett seemed the type to be familiar with untraceable poisons.

I bolted inside and upstairs to get on my street clothes. It was way past the season for bare legs on the street, so I put on pantyhose for the first time since May. I had to go out by the highway to the All Mart. As I exited the alley, I noticed Hugh's Volvo was still in the driveway. I knew he had taught through the summer and I wasn't familiar with holidays over at the college. I drove by his house slowly. Yep, the windshield looked like it was barely holding with all the cracks. It definitely needed replacing. You'd have to go clear to Charlottesville to find a Volvo place with the right parts. I passed Lib, waved and gave a hand signal for her to call me. I wanted to relay the conversation I had with Spookay,Pookay/Puckett earlier.

When I reached the end of the town road, three other cars were stopped ahead of me. Friday traffic was appalling and I wondered if maybe one of the colleges had something going on. It took forever and a day to get up to the stop sign. The big tractor trailers kept going in and out of the truck wash. They were every bit as long as the width of town road. They blocked all view from our side of the road. I was going to stand up with Estelle at council meeting Monday and tell about the length of time it took me to get to the All Mart today. I decided to speak to the All Mart manager and suggest her business would benefit from a traffic light too. I would offer to give her a ride to the meeting Monday. That way it wouldn't just be citizens who would benefit. Shoot, I should stop by the Ye Olde Pickle Barrel and get the Snickelfritzes interested. I hadn't heard a peep out of them since way before the polka dots.

I stopped at the Pickle Barrel first and spoke with Vicky Snickelfritz. She was awkwardly friendly but said she would tell her husband she thought it was a worth considering. The All Mart was my next stop. The manager there was completely on the same page as me. She had almost hit a big truck twice in the last month. She agreed it would help business to break up the bottleneck with a traffic light. Otherwise, the tractor trailers were going to run roughshod over everybody else trying to exit or enter town road.

Betty McMinn walked by as I finished my conversation with the All Mart manager. I smiled cautiously at her, she was one of the enemy. I had a little pang of sympathy for her, knowing her husband might have been having a thing with Darla.

She spoke first, "Hello Mrs. Adams, how are you today?" "Please, call me Tiggy. I thought to myself, "But please don't call me often"

She said she was sorry I had misunderstood the agenda of the Historical

Committee. I assured her the very fact our deeds did not mention any covenants or rules was because zoning laws sufficed.

"Betty, that should have been a dead giveaway we needed to be consulted personally before instituting all y'all's restrictions." Then I caught her off guard and asked her what had happened to her husband's windshield.

"Oh that. Hugh was hit by a large rock on the highway the other night. He was going to the night deposit with the coins from the truck wash." I bit my lip and thought twice.

"Well, how in the world is he going to get it fixed around here?"

Then she told me he was going to drop it off early on Saturday at a place in Charlottesville.

"I suppose he'll have to leave at the crack of dawn, won't he?"

Betty said he had to be at the auto glass place by six A.M. in order to get the car back in one day. I suggested they might try the people who come to your house and replace broken windshields. I had seen an ad for them on television recently. "Betty, they claim to be approved for foreign cars."

She stuck her nose up over that.

"Oh no, only a specialist can replace the type of safety glass standard on a Volvo."

"Suit yourself." I told her and excused myself.

When I got back to town and headed down Beverley, a big parcel truck was parked in front of John and Joanna Blake's. I pulled in front of my house to check if my mail had come. I scooted over the seat to open the mailbox and the parcel delivery guy came over to my driver's window.

"Hello Ma'am, I have a perishable delivery of seafood for your neighbor. Could you sign for it so I won't have to come back to this block? I've got a lot of deliveries today." I said sure and told him I was going around to park in back.

"I'll meet you at my front door in just a minute." He thanked me and went back across to his truck. I brought my frozen stuff in and left the other items in the car for the time being. After I signed for the Blake's package I would finish unloading.

I signed the etch-a-sketch thingy from the parcel service with my name. As I looked at the label from the place in Florida I saw a mistake on the label. It startled me a second. The package was addressed to John Fisher. I looked at it again, thinking I was seeing things. It definitely said, John Fisher and the address was correct. I didn't even want to take it in my house with that name and address on it. John Fisher and Halcey Ann had been dead a long time. Maybe the parcel man saw Fisher/Blake and changed the label. I took it inside and stuck it in my fridge. I called the Blake's phone and left a message for them to call me. I decided to call Hazel, she had a mind like a steel trap. She was busy, so I asked her to call me back as soon as possible.

"And Hazel, call me from your office. I want this to be between you and me for now."

She answered in a slow and deliberate way, "*O.K.* Tiggy."

I had time to get the rest of my groceries and put them away. I also had time to walk Pookie out to the alley before Hazel called me back.

"Sorry Tiggy, it's Friday and there are people from everywhere but "Ishkooda" here to see the polka dot houses." Well does that qualify me for a discount next time?"

She laughed, "How about free coffee from now on?" I told her that would work.

"Now Tiggy, let's cut to the chase. What are you being so mysterious about?"

I asked her to try and remember everything she could about what John and Joanna had asked her about, concerning Mattie and John Fisher. Hazel was able to recall they had questions about what people thought about John. Who did all the furniture belong to in the house. Did folks like Mattie. What was she like. "Now think Hazel, did either of them ever mention Mattie's cousin, Halcey Ann?"

"No Tiggy, they only asked about John and whether or not the story was true about why he and Mattie divorced."

I told her what had happened with the parcel delivery. "Hazel, you don't think he could be that son of John and Halcey Ann's do you?"

"Well, he is the right age Tiggy. But why not just come out and tell people? Wasn't the heir of John's supposed to get half the proceeds from the house after Madeline died?"

"Isn't that why she didn't have to sell the house when they divorced?"

I told her it was in Mattie and John's divorce decree that Mattie had life estate.

"But Hazel, remember Shelby tried to contact the heir down south. She told Lib that some lawyer down there was to handle the property. Shelby was bent out of shape they were not going to pay a realtor. Maybe this is just some kind of weird thing from the outer limits or something.

"Tiggy, the American Parcel Service doesn't deliver to dead people."

"Hazel, not a word of this to anybody until I can sort it out and I don't mean maybe!"

"Cross my heart, eyes and legs!" The mental picture of a plump, middle age woman, with eyes and legs crossed was vivid.

I was almost through supper before the phone rang. I grabbed it on the first ring. It was reporter from a paper in Harrisonburg. As exciting as it was, I didn't want to miss the call from John and Joanna. After I gave him my little spiel, I hung up and went to look out my living room window. I remembered we would need to change our clocks tonight because we would be going off Daylight Savings time. Spring forward, fall back, I told myself. The house was still dark but I dialed their number again. The answering machine came on. Sugar, what if they have gone out of town this weekend? I was about to bust a gut to find out what I didn't already know.

I decided to look for my electric timers while I had the time. I wanted to set my coffee pot on a timer if I could find the instructions. The timing devices were a neighborhood staple at Christmas time. Every citizen on Sherwood Ave set them to go on at five thirty in the afternoon. It was like a ceremony, to come home at dark to all our strings of colored lights. I had recently bought lights resembling icicles for the front of the porch. I started digging in the top of the hall closet. I found my most recent purchase from last Christmas. It was a little tree with a motion sensor. As soon as you approached it, it would sing to you. It was loud but children enjoyed it. Pookie liked to attack it. That usually brought side splitting laughter to kids. I set the tree on the kitchen counter. I remembered then the weather report had predicted a sixty percent chance of rain for tonight. Rather than take a chance getting caught in the rain, I would just let Pookie out in the yard instead of going for a walk.

Before I knew it, I was fiddling with the timers. I thought I would try and set a timer for my coffee machine first. When I looked down at Pookie she was wagging her tail and barking at the tree on the counter. I looked down at her.

"Let's plug up your favorite singing tree and you can attack it when you go out in the yard tonight."

I picked up the tree and set it under my back door overhang. My plug by the back door was sticky with spider webs so I got my rubber glove by the sink and opened it up. I plugged the tree in and let Pookie out. As soon as it detected Pookie's movement, it began moving and singing. The motion of the tree suddenly displayed its felt face. The face belted out a song with a loud, country sort of voice. I let 'Santa Claus is Coming To Town' play through. Pookie barked and lunged at it without actually touching it. I laughed a good one over that.

"On second thought, we need to walk across the street before it rains tonight.

I took her out the front on her leash. There was a light on in the front of Mattie's old house. I knocked and knocked but there was no answer. Pookie and I started to walk around the house but it started to rain in large, stinging drops. We ran back across the street and got inside quickly. I remembered to lock the back door as I came into the kitchen. I closed the downstairs windows and began trying to set a timer for my coffee pot again. I wasn't sure if my coffee would start at five thirty in the morning or five thirty tomorrow evening. The doggone thing was so complicated.

"There precious, maybe when we get back from our walk tomorrow morning, coffee will be waiting for us."

I tried John and Joanna one more time but there was no answer. There was nothing on television worth watching so I decided to turn in early. When I walked by the living room, I stopped at the desk in there to look for old pictures. There on the top of the box of photos was an old Hill and Dale garden party picture. It was of me, Archie, Lib and Gordy, Lilly and Walter and Mattie and John. I thought back to the day some months back when I was looking for photos of Lib's boxwoods. Then I remembered like a bolt of lightning had struck. I felt like I had just seen John Fisher the day I first looked back at the pictures. I wasn't crazy and I didn't have bats in the belfry. I had seen John Fisher, John Fisher Junior! Just then, there was a knock on the door. Pookie sniffed at the door and half-heartedly barked. I figured whoever it was had a friendly smell even though her tail wasn't wagging. I looked through the peep as I opened the door. It was John Fisher, John Fisher Jr. I stood there and invited him in. He was obviously awkward, in his hand was a parcel notice.

"Hello Mrs. Adams, I sure appreciate you accepting our package. We went out to dinner and did some shopping before coming home tonight. The traffic was nonstop down the state road. I think you and your friends have put us on the map."

I smiled at him. "You sit down over there,(I pointed to the living room sofa) and I'll get your package as soon as we have a little neighborly talk. I think you know what I want to ask you."

He didn't answer verbally, but took a deep breath for some kind of invisible strength. I went over to my living room desk and brought the box of photos and placed them in his hand.

He sat there staring at the top photo with Mattie and John. I gave him a minute to look at the picture. Then he began talking at the same time as me. I started to ask him how long he had planned on keeping his identity secret. He sat silently, all flushed as I said, "You first John." I seldom make that allowance.

"Well, may I call you Tiggy?"

"Please do, that's what your father called me."

"As you know, Mom and Dad didn't exactly get together under the right circumstances."

I didn't register any opinion on my face.

"The thing is, my grandfather and grandmother were good to me. They were too forgiving sometimes, or should I say unwilling to take a stand on anything. I was taught by Pop Pop only God can judge. My grandfather believed in turning the other cheek. I felt resentment towards them because they were so wishy washy. My grandfather did not inspire any confidence in me. The reason for this insecurity was due to Pop Pop's attitude towards the people who caused the wreck that killed my parents."

I interrupted him to say maybe his grandparents didn't want him to be bitter. He looked a little startled at me.

John then explained his apprehension towards his grandfather. It seems his grandfather had a visit from the father of one of the college kids who moved the road equipment. "The man and his wife belonged to Pop Pop's church. Now, this was a few days after the wreck and they were unaware I was the grandson of their minister. Remember, my grandfather was a minister." I nodded.

"Tiggy, I overheard or rather I was eavesdropping and heard the conversation. The man admitted his son was one of the people involved in moving the bulldozer to the middle of the road. My grandfather told them not to feel guilty because human beings make mistakes. He suggested the man bring all the culprits to his office so they could say they were sorry to the victim's son. The father said he had told his son it wasn't completely their fault because the road equipment was left with a key under the seat. My grandfather never confronted the man with the devastation his son had caused me. Nor did he appeal strongly enough for the young men to have some remorse. He did not say a word about me being the orphaned son. I always thought it was because the man donated a lot of money to Pop Pop's church. I came here after Mattie Fisher died to place the house I'd inherited up for sale. I fell in love with the area and decided to apply for a job here. I wanted to be accepted before I revealed who I was. My wife has always gone by her maiden name of Blake and that fit with my plan of anonymity. I have come to terms with what happened to my mother and father since the night of the Labor Day party. I now live by the phrase of the Alcoholics Anonymous people. I have let go and let God, as my grandfather would have wanted me to."

"John, now I've got to ask you a serious question and I want a truthful answer."

He told me to ask away.

"Did you know who Hugh McMinn was before you came here?" "Actually, I knew the name of his friend that was involved. It was the father of Hugh's friend, who came for counseling from my grandfather. There were three who set up the circumstances of Mom and Dad's accident. It wasn't until the block party, I even knew Mr. McMinn had gone to school in Tampa. Maybe he was guilty of causing a different accident then the one that killed my parents. Somehow I doubt it. Hugh's story was just too close to home."

I told John that was true in more ways than one. He was able to chuckle and lighten up after that. Then, I told him to keep my box of pictures for a few days.

"Look through all the pictures John, at your leisure and keep any you find of your father."

Just then, Joanna showed up at the door. Pookie went to the door and sniffed. I looked out and saw who it was, then let her in.

"Hi Mrs. Adams." Then she asked John, "Do you know what time it is?"

"I've told Mrs. Adams everything."

"I think it should be kept between you guys. Mr. McMinn is not very likeable and I don't want him trying to make nice nice with us."

I said, "Hey, maybe if you let him know the past is across the street he'll get the heck out of Dodge. Good riddance to him, even though he already did all the damage he could. He is the brains behind getting the Historical Committee written into city statutes."

Joanna said, "I don't think he has a smidgen of selflessness in his body. The way he laughed about the car smashed like an accordion. How it was their mistake to drive too fast. How will anybody ever know if John's parents were driving above the speed limit?"

"I guess I'll have to work on my own forgiveness for Hugh along with y'all. It must haunt him in some way."

John told me he was extremely tired and needed to get some sleep. He took Joanna's hand as she led him onto the front porch. His parting words were, "I feel like "Atlas shrugged", I belong here and apparently Mattie thought so too. She left her part of the house to me. Did you know she did that?"

"No, but just when I think I know everything, it just so happens I don't. John, you not only belong here, but you have taught this old lady a few things tonight. I'm not saying I'm gonna put the incomers on my Christmas card list, but I won't waste time holding a grudge for them anymore. I wished him and Joanna goodnight, then I locked the door after them. I left the porch light on so they could see the walkway.

Pookie and I fell asleep fast that night, a steady rain falling to relax us. I had no sooner gotten to sleep, when the sensor went off on the little Christmas tree. I forgot I'd left it on the back stoop. Around two A.M., it activated with the tune of 'Santa Claus Is Coming To Town'. I awoke to the song as it played, "You better watch out, you better not cry." Pookie was already at the back door going ballistic with her barking. I grabbed the phone and called the police.

"This is Mrs. Archie Adams and I want to report a prowler." The dispatcher that answered was the slug that Lilly and I had encountered before. It was the woman with the personality of a limp dish rag. Lilly and I had dealt with her after the McMinn dog attacked Beaucoup.

"Oh yes, you're Mrs. Tiggy Adams. 305 Sherwood Ave, we know the address well."

10 ANSWERS AND QUESTIONS

Needless to say, I wasn't about to go downstairs until I knew the police had arrived. I didn't try to hush up Pookie either. It made more sense to just let her do her job. The tree quit singing after what seemed an eternal three minutes. Pookie ceased to bark and laid at the back door sniffing loudly. She sounded like someone who'd just watched a sad movie. Soon there was a knock on the front door and the tree out back began singing again. I looked out the second floor window and saw a patrol car in front. I saw a car with lights on in the alley behind me, but couldn't tell if it was a police car. I wasn't sure whether to pick door number one or door number two. Pookie's barking tape was going full volume at the same time. I hollered as I came down the stairs, "Just a minute!" It was enough commotion to make a preacher cuss.

I grabbed up Pookie and forced her into the guest bath under the stairs. I opened the front door and motioned for them to come inside.

"Excuse me officer, I'm going to see who is at the back door."

"Ma'am, that's gonna be officer King out back."

He said this as I walked to the back door. I let the officer in at the kitchen door and he looked at me in acknowledgement. However, he was intently speaking into his collar microphone. I stepped to the back stoop and jerked the plug out from the singing Christmas tree. I wasn't sure if I wanted to hug that tree or throw it against the fence. The officer from the front was now in the doorway of the kitchen, listening to the other officer talking to his collar. I overheard the officer talking on the walkie talkie collar.

"That's right, one set, the ground is soft enough from the rain to get casts. How many signs so far?"

I so wanted to ask the police officer what in the world he was talking about. What kind of sign? A real one, maybe some psychic sign? I didn't want to answer any questions, I wanted to ask them. Then the other officer from the front door asked me if we could sit down somewhere with enough light for writing.

As we sat down in the living room, the officer began to question me. He wanted to know the obvious, like; whether or not I had heard anything unusual before notifying the police. Then the other officer from the back said he had to leave. He asked me to follow him to the back door.

"Ma'am, another officer will be here shortly to take a cast of the footprints left in your yard. The rain tonight has enabled us to distinguish your prints from others. I'd like to request that you keep the area from foot traffic of any kind until the evidence officer is finished. Could you tell me who has recently been in your back yard?"

"Just Pookie and I. I stay on the stepping stones, there are landmines out in the back if you get my drift."

He asked me to step out to the back yard for a look. The officer showed me a set of footprints that were obviously not mine. They were made by those tennis shoes young people wear. The ones with fancy tread work and obscenely priced. None of my fixit people wore such shoes, so it was easy to identify them as out of the ordinary. The way the prints were laid out was odd. It appeared someone had come through my unlocked gate, run across the back corner of the yard and then straight over the fence.

I said out loud to myself and the officer, "Why would someone want to run through my back yard and climb the fence to the front?"

"We may have an answer to that question soon.

"I don't mind answering your questions a bit. Would you answer one for me?"

"If I can Ma'am."

"What kind of signs were you talking about earlier?"

"Oh, that. Well, it seems somebody, probably kids, are going around town stealing stop signs. The stop sign on the street behind you has been stolen as have numerous others around town."

"Oh, now it makes sense. You think it was kids and they probably used my yard to stay out of sight- huh?"

"That seems likely Maam."

The other officer came to the back door and said he couldn't stay to question me. He told the back door officer there was some kind of thing called a "ten fifty". This confused me because it was nearly two fifty by the living room clock.

Both the officers started getting audible messages from their waist walkie talkies. They left my house like they'd been shot out of a cannon. I hollered after the one going out the front. "I guess this means I'm in no danger."

I was so wide awake from all the excitement I decided to make myself a cup of decaf. While the coffee was brewing I called my daughter Tigley, in Boone, North Carolina. She answered on the first ring and I was grateful someone cared to hear about what I had just been through. We talked a few minutes and I promised to write her and send her any pictures or write up in our local paper. After hanging up from Tigley, I locked all the doors front and back. I heard sirens off in the distance. I decided to put on the TV. When my coffee was done, I saw a lady officer come through my back gate with a plastic box. Pookie's bark button turned on and by now I wanted to muzzle her. I went to the door holding her.

"Don't mind the dog, I'll keep her inside."

The lady asked me to fill up her empty gallon milk jug with water. I filled it and gave it back. I watched her mix the water and plaster. Then she poured the mixture in the footprints.

I told her if there was nothing else, I was going to lock up for the night but I would leave my floodlights on. She thanked me and said she wouldn't need anything else. She took about twenty minutes to do whatever she had to do. Pookie sniffed at the back door at least that long. I must have watched almost an hour of television, but there was no break in the programming for a special news report or anything like that. I decided to go on to bed. The Saturday paper would be here soon enough and maybe they would have the story and all the details.

"Well Pooks, lets go back to bed and get some rest, looks like all the excitement is over for one day."

The next morning, I awoke to Pookie nuzzling me. She was patient with me as I dressed for walking. We headed out the back door and through the alley. We were the only ones out, no joggers or crash test dummies. Then I spied Lilly with Jenny and Beaucoup.

"Oh Tiggy, I wasn't sure you'd be out this morning with all the news."

"You mean about the stop signs?"

"Partly Tiggy, but it's more serious than just missin stop signs."

"More serious in what way?" Lilly got dramatic on me.

"Oh dear, you don't mean I'm the first to tell you?!"

I stood there about to lose patience but her eyes were so pained.

"Hugh McMinn is in intensive care at county Hospital. He was on his way last night to pick up his night deposit from the coin machines at the truck wash. He was driving the town road and never stopped at the intersection because the stop sign was gone. He ran right into one of the trucks coming out of his own truck wash."

"How did he do that Lilly? Was the rain too heavy for him to see where the road ended or something?"

"Tiggy, even with head lights on you don't know you're at the intersection unless you've driven the road as many years as you and I have. They tried to steal the stop sign where the town road intersects with the state road. Apparently they couldn't get it out of the ground, so they just knocked it down where you couldn't see it."

I must have looked like a bucket of ice water had just been dumped on my head. I couldn't find my voice for a moment. "Tiggy, are you alright?"

"I called the police last night because I had a prowler and they told me about the signs. They found a set of strange footprints in my back yard which is probably connected to the thefts. Then, a lady policeman came to my back yard to make a mold of the prints for evidence too. Have they caught who stole the signs?" "No, but the newspaper and the television man said there were four stop signs and one speed limit sign taken last night. Folks are 'sposed to be on the lookout for anybody in possession of the signs."

"Lilly, I think I know when the wreck happened. It happened around two thirty in the morning."

"The paper didn't say what time the wreck happened."

I decided to turn around and go back home to read my paper. I told Lilly to come over for coffee after she got Jenny and Beaucoup settled.

"I'm calling Estelle and Lib too. I have more news besides Hugh's wreck to tell you about."

Lilly said she would be at my house ASAP. When I reached my front door and opened it, I smelled freshly brewed coffee. I felt triumphant I had set the timer correctly. I need help to change a light bulb but I can quote Shakespeare. I was so proud of myself for doing something mechanical. I looked down at Pookie.

"One small step for man, one giant leap for mankind."

No, it wasn't on the par with landing on the moon, but now I had the confidence to buy a DVD player. I dug around my cabinet for my insulated carafe, because I was going to need a full pot of coffee for the girls.

A few minutes after I started the second pot of coffee, I dialed Estelle. She sounded half asleep.

"Estelle, I've got coffee going. Don't read the paper or do anything til you get over here. Have I got a shockeroo for you!"

"Gimme a minute to brush my teeth and dress, B,Y."

I hung up to call Lib but she opened my front door just as I started to dial.

"Tiggy! Tiggy!" she hollered.

"I already heard about the wreck Lib. Lilly and Estelle are on their way over. There's more than news about Hugh McMinn. There's something I've got to tell all y'all about Hugh McMinn and John Fisher!"

Lib looked at me like I'd completely lost my mind.

The words were no sooner out of my mouth when there was a knock on the front door. Pookie beat me to the door and barked only once. I opened the door to find John Fisher Jr.. I saw Lib crane her neck to see who it was.

"Tiggy, did you hear? Is he going to be O.K.?"

"I don't know yet. All my friends are headed over here. They were your father's friends too." He looked sheepishly towards Lib.

"Can I be the one to tell them?"

I told him sure and had him follow me to the kitchen. Estelle and Lilly both came through the front door as we were halfway to the kitchen.

"Good morning all, you know my neighbor John Fisher. John this is Lilly Wiley and Estelle Gwaltney. The lady with her jaw on the floor is Lib Armstrong."

I did hate to upstage poor John, but it certainly got him everybody's undivided attention. I gestured for everybody to sit down. I went over to the counter and poured coffee for everyone. As I handed each person a cup, John began to explain the entire story. After he had filled in every last detail of how he came to be in Mountain Empire, Estelle was the first to speak.

"How lovely that Mattie left her part of the house to you." Lib said, "I always felt like I'd met you somewhere before. I guess I did in some sort of way."

John turned to me and the others, "I would like to put everything behind me. If Hugh is one of the guys responsible for Mom and Dad's wreck, I would like to tell him I forgive him."

Lib put her hand on his shoulder, "John, it sounds like it was him. If you can do that it will free you."

I asked, "Has the news said anything about how Hugh is?" They each said they hadn't heard. I turned on my television to the local station. There were cartoons on and no news programs so I hit the mute button. John asked all of us to keep the secret until he could speak to Hugh.

I told him, "This kitchen is the keeper of many secrets. Yours are now safe here too."

Then John left and we sat there chewing on everything that had happened. I suggested that one of us call Betty and find out about Hugh. Lib offered to call Shelby since she was friendly with them. Shelby told Lib Hugh had gone into a coma. We all remarked we needed to have everybody pray for Hugh at church. Then we drank another pot of coffee together. We all discussed how our lives had changed since the incomers. Some of it good and some of it bad. Everybody but Estelle left after a little while. When we were alone in the kitchen, Estelle said she had a few secrets to leave in the kitchen too.

That got my attention so I sat across from her and said, "Let's hear it."

"Pete and Darla are getting back together. Her divorce from Bobby will be final in a few weeks."

Then she gave me all the sordid details that led up to the reconciliation. I darn near got shock fatigue that morning. I listened to the most unbelievable story involving trouble and Darla. Maybe I should rephrase and say it was typical of anything to do with Darla. As it turned out, Pete was the one who had put the marine grease on Bobby's ladders and sawhorses. Estelle said he was furious over Bobby taking Darla away from him. When the neighbors complained about all of Bobby's construction equipment in the alley Pete felt safe in acting out his aggression. That wasn't all he did either. When Darla left for Memphis with the girls for two weeks, Pete used the key left outside to gain entry. He purposely rubbed car wax under the back entry door mat and all over the floor of the entrance. That caused Bobby to nearly break his neck. The story about the cleaning lady making the mistake was just that, a story. Bobby was too proud to admit someone had gotten the best of him.

"Estelle, what about Darla and Bill Puckett?

Pete didn't have anything to do with the bad hot water heater did he?"

"Sort of. You see, Mrs. Puckett specifically asked him to order that hot water heater. She told him it was on sale and she wanted it for the master bath. She had Carter Crawford install it the day she went to the beach with her son. Pete looked it up on the computer to see what the sale price was and found out there was a kit that had to be installed with the flue baffles or the warranty was no good. He called Mrs. Puckett and informed her the kit was free but only an experienced plumber would be able to follow the installation instructions."

"I knew it! That woman wanted to kill Bill and get away with it!"

"But Tiggy, the company didn't say why the gas baffles had to have the extra kit. Only the web site for consumer product safety did."

"Estelle, you can't tell me that Puckett woman didn't do her homework before trying to do in her husband."

"Tiggy, I never thought of it that way. She is such a sour, temperamental, person who knows what she's capable of. She quit speaking to one of her friends here for no legitimate reason. Carter said she screams like a banshee at her husband and son over nothing. But murder, can someone go from being fractious to homicidal?"

"Estelle, if they leave their emotions unchecked, a person can go to all kind of extremes."

Estelle switched back to the subject of Pete and Darla. She told me when Pete admitted to the pranks against Bobby, Darla began cozying up to him.

"Oh, I get it Estelle, Darla likes a bad boy."

Estelle said Darla asked him if he had beat on Hugh McMinn's car.

"Tiggy, Pete told me he wasn't aware of anything to do with Hugh's car. Thinking he was on a roll with Darla, he confessed to something he didn't do, all for love."

Then Estelle asked me if I knew anything about Hugh's car. I told her about the incident out in the alley and my calling the police. Estelle said she was amazed that all Pete had to do in getting Darla back was appear incorrigible. I listened as cautiously as possible, trying to keep my opinions out of the conversation. Poor Pete, he was headed back to the altar with a woman that had turned him into a court jester. Estelle looked at her watch and told me she had to run. I told her I was happy for her and Pete. That wasn't a total lie, just half the truth. All the revelations from Estelle remained in my kitchen that day. A lot of questions were answered that morning. Speculation remained about a lot of other things that had happened since the incomers.

Two months later, the Historical Review Committee went ahead with their open house and walking tour. The polka dots were removed with the provision our way of decorating would not be called into question. The tour was such a success, a big advertising firm on Wall Street began paying us on Sherwood Ave for the right to shoot commercials in our neighborhood. A woman who worked for the ad agency found us by accident. She had stopped out by the highway and saw the billboard promoting the open house. The rest, as we say, is history and in a historical district to boot! We were soon the scene for ads touting everything from mortgages to drain cleaners.

The second year after the advertisements were shot, a scene for the movie 'Gods and Generals' was made on Sherwood. The shooting of the movie was the event which turned a few incomers into citizens. After all, it was the incomers who put us on the map with the open house and walking tour. It was only fair to make them citizens. Another movie scene was filmed after that too. It required only cars from the late fifties and early sixties. The Christmas scene had to be staged with decorations from the early fifties and sixties. Mrs. Puckett wanted her house on Central Avenue to be in the movie to the point of desperation. She turned from a tiger to a lamb towards Mary Lou Knorr and all of us. You see, we are the ones who loaned her the "period" decorations she needed in order to be included in the movie shoot. The very decorations she tried to zone away from our neighborhood. It was hysterical to see her front walkway lined with big, faded candy canes. The two sun faded, four foot toy soldiers on either side of her front door were a loan from me, thank you very much! The cars from the right period were brought in by the movie people. You might have seen our homes in Mountain Empire, Virginia and been unaware of it.

Some of the biggest questions about what happened before Hugh McMinn's accident have never been answered. I can only tell you what I know. No one ever confessed to supplying the fans that caused Bill Nibruska's house to burn down. No doubt it was someone trying to be helpful. I'll always think it was Bobby Tatum that tried to destroy Hugh McMinn's windshield. As for the 'it' caller, my gut tells me it was Mrs. Puckett. Maybe it was Pete, but if he was willing to admit all the other things why not the crank calls? I could never discuss the 'it' caller with any of my friends. That would have revealed my foreknowledge of Darla and Bill Puckett fooling around. The stop sign thief or thieves which caused Hugh's accident were never caught. I wrote my daughter a long letter the day after Hugh's accident. There was no other way to tell her everything and keep it in order. Letters are good that way. I don't mind sharing part of that letter with you:

Dear Tigley,

I know you are wondering about the frantic call last night. The footprints the police found may have been connected to the stop sign theft that caused Hugh McMinn's car wreck. You remember he is the one I told you about. He is responsible for that Historical Review Committee. As you will recall, he joked about some people in Tampa dying in a wreck he was responsible for causing. When he was in college, he and some friends moved a bulldozer into the middle of a blind spot in the road. Remember, Mattie Fisher's first husband was killed in Tampa from a car wreck during the same period. A wreck caused by someone moving a bulldozer to the middle of the road. The fact Hugh admitted at our Labor Day party to causing a fatal wreck in Tampa as a young person is ironic. (Of course he was drunk when he admitted this awful deed) It was probably a college kid to blame for Hugh's wreck too. I've never believed in that karma stuff. I believe you reap what you sow, just like it says in the Bible.

There were other factors which contributed to Hugh's accident. The rain and the busted windshield on his car probably didn't help. It was an angry husband who busted his windshield, by the way. The man was just asking for trouble, if you ask me. John Fisher Jr. was noble enough to pay a visit to Hugh while he was in a comatose state. John Jr. wanted him to know he had no grudge for the death of his father and mother. John Fisher Jr. and his wife Joanna are such dear neighbors to Lilly, Lib, Estelle and I. Anyway, I know you will want to know if Hugh McMinn made it out of the coma alright. Darn it sweetie, I'll continue in a minute. Someone is at the front door and you know how loudly

Pookie can bark.

ABOUT THE AUTHOR

Channing Belle Grove is a mother and grandmother, a former teacher, real estate agent and forever a military wife.

Made in the USA
Monee, IL
10 June 2022